THE DEMONIC

LEE MOUNTFORD

For my wife, Michelle.

FREE BOOKS

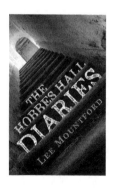

Want two free horror stories written by me? Sign up to my mailing list and receive your free copy of *The Hobbes Hall Diaries* and *The Demon of Dunton Hall* (prequel to The Demonic) directly to your email address.

And that's just the start—as a thank you for your support, I plan on giving away as much free stuff to my readers as I can. To sign up just go to my website and get your free stories.

www.leemountford.com

1

——————

'DEATH IS A PART OF LIFE,' Jon said. 'And, unfortunately, it comes to us all.'

While a true enough statement, the topic of discussion —of life and death—wasn't one Danni Morgan wanted to be having right now.

Not now.

The family was packed into the large SUV, along with provisions for the weekend, and heading towards her hometown of Bishops Hill.

A place she hadn't been back to in a long time. Not since that fateful night.

A place she never thought she would return to.

And yet, here she was, making the two hundred-and-fifty-mile trip, all so she could lay to rest a father she hadn't spoken to in twenty years.

'Very profound, Dad,' said Danni's teenage daughter, Leah, from the back seat. Most of the girl's attention was focused on her smart phone. 'I can already tell this trip is going to be fun.'

'Funerals aren't supposed to be fun,' said her younger brother, Alex, from the seat beside her.

'And what about car trips?' Leah asked. 'Can those be fun?'

'I only asked what happened to him,' Alex said.

'And you were told,' she replied. 'Can we change the subject now?'

'Yeah, that's not a bad idea,' Danni said. She and Leah were a lot alike in many respects, and being uncomfortable around the topic of death was just one of many traits they shared. Her husband Jon, and their son Alex, were different; more open to its discussion but, dare she say, a little more cold in how they approached it. Alex's line of thinking, she knew, was very much moulded and shaped by his father's.

The boy adored him.

As well he should.

Normally after the loss of a parent, a child would be in mourning. But with Danni, it was different; there was a fucking good reason they hadn't spoken for such a long time.

Even so, she was feeling *something*, but she just couldn't put her finger on what that something was. Things felt somehow... unfinished. And now, it seemed, nothing would ever be resolved. Maybe that wasn't such a bad thing.

She didn't want these scars to heal.

She didn't want that man finding any kind of forgiveness, or peace, before death.

And maybe this was its own kind of closure. The last thing anchoring Danni to her old life was now gone.

Though that wasn't strictly true, was it? There was still one thing that existed linking her back to Bishops Hill.

Her family home.

The one she grew up in, and had just inherited. She felt

her husband's hand fall gently to her knee. It gave a reassuring squeeze.

'Sorry, hun,' he said, letting his gaze drift from the road for a moment to meet her eyes. 'It was an insensitive thing to be talking about.'

'It's okay,' she replied, putting her hand on his. 'I would just prefer if things were a little lighter. Our car trips used to be fun. What happened to things like *I-Spy*?'

Leah let out a laugh. 'I think we outgrew it, Mom.'

'Nonsense,' Jon cut in. 'You never outgrow *I-Spy*.'

'Then you start,' Danni said, happy to redirect the conversation.

'And don't make it anything stupid, Dad,' Alex said. 'I remember the whole Honda Civic fiasco.'

'Honda begins with the letter H,' Jon said, a slight smile creeping across his lips. 'So it didn't break any rules.'

'But we passed it before we had a chance to guess,' Leah cut in. 'It was so unfair.'

'Then you need to be more observant and quicker with your answers,' he said. 'Now, I spy with my little eye...'

THE GAME HAD BEEN fun and kept them occupied for about an hour until their first service stop. They had been travelling for just under two hours when they pulled off the motorway and were a little under halfway through the journey. It was good to get out of the car, breathe in the fresh air, and stretch their legs.

The SUV was a great vehicle for the family: brand new, very spacious, and packed with the latest gadgets and technology—though Jon had insisted on stopping short of getting television sets in the back of the headrests—but no matter how comfortable it was, being stuck in the same seated position and enclosed space for too long would always seize the joints and numb the mind.

Jon topped up the tank at the pump, then pulled the vehicle into a free space close to the large service facility. The building had high glazed facades and white steel sections—its design reminded Danni more of an airport than a motorway service station. Jon pulled into one of the disabled bays and, before they all disembarked, put the parking badge on the dashboard. Leah was the first to help her brother with his crutches.

'I don't think I need them,' he said. 'It's not far.'

'Just take them for now,' Leah said, 'and if you can go without, I'll carry them.'

Another trait Danni shared with her daughter: being fiercely protective of the ones she loved. As the eldest of the two, Leah had taken the role of protector, and though they bickered occasionally, nothing could deter her in that role. And, to Alex's credit, he didn't seem to mind having a girl look out for him. Whilst independent of mind, he knew that sometimes he needed physical help and seemed comfortable accepting it from his sister. Of all the things Danni had to offer the world, none made her as proud as her children. Watching these two grow into strong, caring, considerate people filled her heart with happiness.

It was also a relief to know that, at least so far, both her and Jon had succeeded as parents.

And she would be damned if she was going to fail as drastically as her own father had.

Though, in truth, she had felt like a failure once before. Not long after Alex was born, he was diagnosed with cerebral palsy—a condition he had since lived with his entire life, not knowing anything different. Danni and Jon were told that it was likely caused by brain development damage during pregnancy. As the one who had carried Alex, Danni had judged herself a failure and the person solely responsible. She felt like she had snatched her son's life away from him before it had even started. No amount of logic, put forward by Jon and the doctors, could change her mind on that.

They hadn't been the one carrying the boy.

It wasn't their job to keep him safe.

They just didn't know.

But as he grew, he adapted, and he coped with the situation. It was never easy: even now Danni would, at times, watch him struggle on without a complaint and her heart would break a little. But as he grew older his personality developed, and it became clear he wouldn't accept much in the way of sympathy.

In fact, he developed a saying: 'It is what it is.' Something he would say with a shrug and a smile.

Even at such a young age, he knew life could sometimes be unfair, and often there was nothing that could be done about it. But he got on with it. Always with a smile.

Alex's condition primarily affected his legs, making walking difficult. He could manage short distances without crutches, but it took effort and wore him down quickly. The crutches helped with greater distance as well as balance. When taking a step, he had to swing his legs, with knees bent inwards, giving the impression that he was wading through waist-high water. People would stare a little, and that always bugged Danni, as it did Leah, but Alex paid it no mind. 'They just aren't used to it,' he would say.

It is what it is.

As much as Danni and Leah shared a lot of traits, there was no doubt that Alex took after his father. They were both measured thinkers and thought before they leapt. Strong-willed, but extremely patient. And Alex had developed his father's thirst for knowledge and desire to learn. His condition meant he couldn't be as active as most boys his age, so to compensate he constantly keep his mind active. Where his sister was always on her smartphone, checking on social media, Alex always had his head in a book—both paper, and his prized e-reader—learning new things.

Jon hoped Alex would follow him into physics and lecturing, but Danni knew Alex had his sights set much higher.

Quite literally.

Many things interested the boy, but nothing engaged his imagination like the mysteries that lay outside of the planet.

Where did we come from?

How do solar systems work?

How close are we to settling on other worlds?

Whenever Danni engaged him with similar questions, she would see an excited light burn in his eyes, and the pitch in his voice jumped up a few levels as he spoke quicker and with more enthusiasm.

'Can't we just grab a burger?' Leah asked as they made their way to the entrance, snapping Danni back from her thoughts.

'No,' Jon said. 'I'm sure we can find something a little healthier than that.'

'We probably can,' she replied, 'but sometimes it's nice to be a little indulgent.'

They walked through the automatic sliding door, and as they did Danni felt a blast of cold air hit her from the cooling unit in the ceiling above. The air danced over her face and she pulled her purple hiking coat tighter around her. It was autumn, not her favourite season, but it seemed the farther north they drove, the colder things got.

Once through the lobby, the interior of the building opened up into a huge, open space that allowed light to spill in from the front wall of glazing. Different store fronts—mainly fast-food chains—hugged the back wall, serving throngs of people, but the bulk of the floor was a sprawling seating area. The smells inside were an odd mix of junk-food grease and the aroma of coffee.

'Okay,' Danni said, taking charge. 'First, toilet break, then we meet back here and decide what we do for food.'

'Agreed,' Jon said, and put a hand onto Alex's shoulder. 'Come on, champ, let's go.'

Danni heard the gentle *click, click, click* of Alex's crutches as he moved. It disappeared as he entered the toilet area with his dad. Given the length of time Alex had been using his crutches, she had grown to associate that fragile sound with him. She knew he would be mad about that if he ever found out—associating him with fragility—but she couldn't help it. It was instinctual.

She wanted to protect him, she wanted to protect all of her family, and the thought of bringing them back to a place that had damaged her felt like a betrayal of that.

But her father was gone now. Danni needed to remember that.

Gone forever.

So why did she have this troubling feeling deep in her gut? Like this was a bad idea. Like she was, somehow, putting her family in danger.

Danni hadn't even wanted to make the trip in the first place. She had hoped to sort everything that needed sorting over the phone, but Jon had pushed her into it.

'Hello? Mom?' Leah said, yet again pulling Danni back from her thoughts. 'Are you still with us?'

'Yeah, sorry,' Danni said, giving her head a shake. 'Was just lost in my own little world for a minute there.'

'Well now that you're back, let's go pee,' Leah said. She linked her arm through Danni's and led her to the toilet.

Still, Danni couldn't shake that feeling of foreboding that weighed on her, and Jon's words from earlier played over in her mind.

Death comes to us all.

2

DANNI FELT her chest tighten a little as they closed in on their destination. The drive had been relatively uneventful, with only one service stop to break up the monotony. Now, however, they were less than ten minutes out according to the onboard satellite navigation, and Jon had already phoned the local solicitors they were dealing with to confirm their imminent arrival.

The representative would meet with them at the house, go over some paperwork, and hand over the keys to Danni's newly inherited property.

One that she did not want.

The knot forming in Danni's gut grew tighter.

She didn't want to deal with what lay ahead, and would have preferred if she could have ignored the whole thing, stayed in London, and have somebody else resolve everything. Let the banks have her family home, for all she cared.

Let it rot.

Anything so she could just carry on with her life as it was now, uninterrupted, and not get dragged back into the past.

After finding out about her father's death—from a heart attack, she was told—Danni had discussed the idea of not going back with Jon. He said that, ultimately, the choice was hers to make, but pushed for her to return.

Jon knew about Danni's rough childhood, or most of it. He was about the only person she had ever opened up to regarding it, and he thought this might be a good way for her to get some kind of closure. She had run from her past long enough, he had said, and this was a way to finally face up to those old ghosts that haunted her.

Danni wasn't convinced.

But, in the end, she had conceded and agreed to return home so she could drop her father's body into the dirt.

The SatNav ordered them to take the next exit from the motorway, and Jon eased the SUV over into the inside lane, ready for the turnoff. This stretch of the motorway was familiar to Danni, and that familiarity was not pleasant. It meant she was close. She knew that just up ahead the slip road would lead them off the motorway, where they would take a left at the roundabout, then carry on for a short while before making a sharp right. This would lead them along Church Lane—a long, winding country road—down a gentle decline. If things were as she remembered them, that road would be flanked on both sides by rolling fields that used to be dotted with sheep, cows, and even goats. It was one of only two roads that led directly into Bishops Hill.

'You okay, hun?' Jon asked, looking over to her.

Danni realised she was holding her breath. She let it out, as gently as she could. 'Yeah, I'm fine. Just strange going back, you know?'

Jon smiled and nodded. 'Yeah,' he said, 'I can imagine. You want to stop somewhere first, give yourself a little time before going to the house?'

Yes, she thought to herself. That's exactly what she wanted. To go somewhere, anywhere, and get a drink she didn't want to drink, or get some food she didn't want to eat, and maybe reconsider this whole trip. Or, better yet, turn the car around right then and just go home.

Her real home, the one she had made for herself.

Not this fading echo of one.

But she knew, deep down, Jon was right about trying to find some kind of closure. Things may now be forever unfinished between Danni and her father, but this would be the closest she would get.

'No,' she eventually said, 'let's keep going.'

And so they did; off the stretch of motorway, left at the roundabout, then a sharp right and down the small, winding road known as Church Lane.

About halfway down the country road, they saw it—all bent and twisted and suffering.

A goat, on the verge of death.

The tarmac beneath it was stained red, and blood pumped from open wounds as the animal tried, and failed, to pull itself upright on its broken limbs.

Jon brought the car to a slow stop and flicked on his hazard lights.

'Oh, God,' Leah said from the back seat.

Not that the girl was religious, none of the family were, but Danni had almost said the same thing, before Leah had beaten her to it. Part of Danni wanted to look away, but she continued to peer through the windshield at the poor animal.

'What is it?' Alex asked, then drew in a sharp intake of breath. 'Is that a goat? Oh, the poor thing.'

'It is,' Jon said. 'It must have come from the fields, gotten through the fence and onto the road. Looks like it was hit by a car or something.'

It seemed these fields were still used for grazing, as Danni remembered, and were littered with the same breed of animals they always had been, though the numbers seemed greatly reduced.

'So someone hit it and then just drove off?' Alex asked, the disgust prevalent in his voice.

'Looks that way,' Jon said.

The goat let out a faint, desperate bleat, and kicked out a leg.

'It's in pain, Dad,' Leah said. 'What do we do? We can't just leave it.'

'And we won't,' Jon said.

'So what do we do?' Leah asked again. 'Are you going to...' she let her voice trail off.

'Kill it? No, I couldn't bring myself to do that,' Jon said, and pulled out his mobile phone. 'But we can always call the police.'

'It's in real pain,' Leah went on.

'I know, hun,' he replied, as gently as he could. 'Hopefully this won't take long.'

Jon typed in the emergency number and lifted the phone to his ear.

'Will it live?' Alex asked.

'I don't know, Son,' Jon said. 'Maybe.'

Danni knew that was a kindness to the boy. The animal was past saving.

Danni concentrated on the goat as her husband got through to the police. It may have been an animal she had no attachment to, but seeing it in such distress made her feel utterly helpless.

'What do you mean, *when you can*?' she heard her

husband say as she tuned back in to his conversation. 'Well, can't you be quick about it? If nothing else, surely this is an accident waiting to happen?' He let out an exacerbated breath. 'Fine,' he eventually said, in a way that meant everything was not fine. He hung up.

'What did they say?' Alex asked.

'Long and short of it? They will send someone out when they are able to.'

'What does that mean?' Danni said. 'Can't they contact the RSPCA?'

'That'll be up to the police,' he said. 'Hopefully they will, but I only got through to the call handlers. They'll pass the info on to the police.'

'So they could be here soon?' Alex asked.

'Might be,' Jon said.

'But likely it will take forever,' Leah added.

'Probably,' Jon answered.

The car fell silent. Danni looked around, half hoping another car would approach, one that could offer assistance, but they had no such luck. They were on their own, on an isolated road that cut its way through fields of nothing, and the only possibility of help lay miles down the road, in the settlement of Bishops Hill. But going for help meant leaving the animal behind, and Danni seriously doubted they would find anyone who would be willing to travel back here to aid with the situation.

So that meant they would have to deal with it. And the only act of kindness she could think of was to try and give the animal some form of comfort in its last moments.

That, or put an end to its misery.

'There,' Jon said, pointing ahead, just to the left. Danni looked, and soon saw it, tucked away among a crop of trees. A house, standing alone in the sea of grass. Upon seeing it, something unlocked in her memory, and she felt stupid not realising it had been here the whole time. It was a place she'd seen many times when passing along this road, but had never known who owned it.

'Maybe someone is in,' Danni said. 'They might be able to help.'

'It looks like a farmhouse,' Alex said. 'Perhaps the goat belonged to them?'

'Look,' Danni said, pointing. 'There's a turning to it, just up ahead.'

'Yeah,' Jon said, nodding. 'Okay, we'll drive up and see if anyone is home.'

'We can't leave the goat here on its own,' Leah said.

'We don't have a choice, hun,' Jon replied. 'There's nothing we can do for it, except get help.'

'Then I'll stay here with it. You go.'

'No,' Jon said, firmly. 'Sorry, Leah, but I'm not having you stand in the middle of the road on your own. Understand?'

'I guess,' she said, crossing her arms. 'But can we be quick?'

'As quick as we can,' Jon said, putting the SUV in gear. He carefully drove around the struggling goat, while it continued its weak bleating.

It took less than a minute to reach the narrow turning in the road, which brought them to little more than a dirt path that ran up to the house. As they drove along the makeshift road, Danni caught sight of a dull, green Landrover—the lower half caked with mud—parked outside, giving her hope that someone was home. The house itself was a low one, single storey, but from the positioning of the windows in the gable and the presence of roof windows, it was clear the second storey was built in the roof space. Its external finish was old brickwork, and had a slate roof, which gave the building an aged, urban quality.

Jon pulled the SUV round and parked it adjacent to the Landrover.

'Wait here,' Jon said, and got out of the car, pulling himself up to his impressive full height. As friendly and amicable as Jon was, Danni knew that, to some, he could cast an imposing presence. Danni knew that, in a place like Bishops Hill, a six-foot-two black man standing on a person's porch would come as quite a surprise. She watched Jon trot up to the front door and knock. As he waited, Danni lowered her window so she could hear any exchange.

It didn't take long for the door to open, revealing a short, stout woman, with frizzy grey hair that spilled out of a loose bun. She seemed like she was getting on in years, but Danni had a feeling she was the type that looked older than she really was. Danni saw a brief look of shock register on the woman's face, which was, thankfully, soon replaced with a smile.

'Can I help?' she asked.

'I hope so,' Jon said. 'My family and I were just driving down the road back there, and we came across an animal that had been hit. It's still alive, but only barely. We didn't know if it was yours, perhaps?'

'What sorta' animal is it?' she asked.

'A goat,' Jon replied.

The woman sighed. 'That's probably ours,' she said. 'We have one that keeps findin' a way through the fence. Lord knows how he does it.'

'Well, we didn't want to just leave it,' Jon said. 'We phoned it in to the police, but I'm not sure they were of the mind to send anyone over.'

'Probably won't,' the woman said, stepping out of the

house. Jon moved aside to let her through. 'They never do—we normally clear everything up. Which is only fair, I suppose. Where is it?'

'Back up the road a little,' Jon said, pointing in the general direction.

'Thanks,' she replied. 'I'll make sure I see to it.'

'Do you think there is anything you can do for it?'

'Not much can be done,' she said with a shrug. 'Except bang it over the head.'

Danni prayed the kids didn't hear that part.

'I see,' Jon said.

'Thanks for lettin' me know, though. Most people would've just drove on. Like the ones that hit it, no doubt.'

'Well, it seemed like the right thing to do.'

'The right thing isn't always the easiest,' she said. 'That's why most don't often do the right thing. You staying in Bishops Hill, or just passing through?' she asked.

'Staying for a little while with my family,' Jon said, gesturing to the car where Danni and the kids sat. The woman didn't look over. Instead, she smiled. Not a warm, friendly smile, but something with a little more purpose. Something a little more... predatory.

'Well, if you ever need anything, you just let me know,' she said. 'Name's Jean.' Jean extended her hand to Jon, and he took it and shook.

'I'm Jon,' he said. 'It was a pleasure to meet you. We need to be going, so I'll leave you to it. Good luck with your animal.'

'Thank you, hun,' she said, and touched the tip of her tongue to her top lip. Danni felt a swell of defensive anger bubble up from her gut. The old bat was shamelessly flirting with her husband.

Danni leaned her head out of the window. 'I think we need to get going, sweetheart.'

Jon turned around and nodded, a definite look of relief on his face, clearly grateful for the assistance. 'Coming.'

He strode back to the car and cast Jean a final wave.

She didn't wave back, just stared, with the corner of her mouth turned up in a half smirk.

Jon got in the car, put it in gear, and drove them back down to the main road.

'So what did she say?' Leah asked.

'The goat is hers,' Jon said.

'And is she going to help it?'

Jon pulled the car onto the road and headed towards Bishops Hill, leaving Jean and her doomed goat behind.

Jon and Danni gave each other a look.

'She's going to do what she can,' Jon said.

They drove on and Danni couldn't help but feel even more apprehensive. Logically, that was understandable, considering the suffering animal they had just seen. Yet, somehow, she felt like she should have expected such a thing.

She sighed.

Welcome home, Danni.

3

THE ROUTE to Danni's childhood home took them straight through the centre of town, and Jon was careful to keep an eye on his wife as they drove, trying to read her facial expressions for signs of worry.

He knew this trip was going to be hard for her, but he also knew it was one she needed to make. He would be by her side the whole time, as he should be, but this was something that, ultimately, she needed to do for herself.

For as long as he had known her, Danni had been friendly and outgoing, but it didn't take him long to notice an inner sadness. Often, when Danni thought no one was paying attention and was lost in contemplation, Jon would see a mournful look creep over her face.

Jon didn't learn the full story of what had happened to her until well after they were married and were expecting Leah. The story shocked and saddened him. He hated the thought of the woman he loved having to go through so much, so early in life. And he didn't blame her for running away. But he also knew that there was a time when you needed to stop running and face up to things.

They drove along a main road that bisected the town, taking them through an area full of simple, red-bricked, terraced houses, complete with small rear yards that were enclosed with high brick walls. Some people sat out on their front steps, most in dressing gowns enjoying a drink in the chilly afternoon air. Farther ahead, he saw a group of youths in caps and tracksuits huddled at a bus-stop, a few of them smoking, a few of them drinking, but all of them trying their best to look tough, mean, and threatening. They all stared at the SUV as it drove past, puffing out their chests and curling their lips into a scowl. Jon had a feeling it was a standard reaction to anything they saw as being different from the norm.

However, Jon kept his judgement at bay, as he often did, knowing everyone's circumstances were different. Still, he couldn't help but feel thankful his children didn't have to grow up in a place like this. He would never say it to Danni, knowing how difficult this trip was for her, but Bishops Hill seemed like it was in its last throes of life.

A dying and forgotten place, ready to fall into obscurity.

They soon passed an old train station; closed and unused. Alex had asked about it as they had driven past, and Danni responded that it had closed before she was even born. She mentioned the line was still in use, taking people through the town, but no trains ever stopped here anymore.

Next, they hit the bottom of a steep hill, with roads branching off to the left and right as they went up, leading to little pockets of housing which were a little nicer than those near the station: semi-detached properties with actual, honest-to-God gardens and lawns. Something of a rarity in this town, it seemed.

At the top of the hill, the road turned sharply to the left, going past a line of low stone bungalows—all terraced—

which, according to Danni, were the remnants of an old farm that was no longer here.

The road then opened up to reveal the hub of the town. The centre of it was taken up with car parking and a few bus stops, and the edges of the centre were lined with shops, takeaway restaurants, and pubs. There was also a large, two-storey, white-rendered building just off the central car park, with a long garden to its front. In this garden stood a tall stone statue of a saluting military man. That was a World War II memorial, according to Danni, and the building was the town hall.

People milled about, going from shop to shop—and pub to pub—looking aimless, without purpose.

Existing without really living.

Jon caught himself—those *were* judgmental thoughts, and not something to be proud of.

They followed the road around the centre. This led them to a steep drop down a hill, and Jon guessed the name of the settlement was due to the town centre being atop the hill. Instead of following the road down, however, they took a sharp right that would lead them out towards their destination.

Jon sensed Danni tense up.

They were close.

They followed the road past more terraced houses, and a long, low, rectangular building, with a flat roof, and walls that consisted of cheap looking plastic panels. This, Danni had said with no pride at all, was her old school.

After this, they broke clear of the built-up area, heading into a clearing of farming fields. Off to the left, a little way ahead, Danni pointed out a building.

'There it is,' she said with a hint of sadness and trepidation. 'Home sweet home.'

Jon noticed something strange about the house on the approach.

As did the children.

'What's that near the house?' Alex asked.

'That's an old mill,' Danni said. 'Left over from when it was a farm.'

The cylindrical stone structure was very distinct and sat to the back of the property's borders, near to a line of trees.

'Looks a little creepy, Mom,' Leah said.

Danni nodded. 'Yeah, it is. Always was.'

'But it's so cool,' Alex added, clearly having a different line of thinking than his sister.

Away from the mill, and standing not-so-proudly, was a detached, two-storey house. While it was clearly not as old as the mill, it stood in a definite state of decline. It was clad in distressed shiplap timber—like no other buildings in town, which were primarily brick and render. It had stained and rotten wooden windows throughout, one of which was a large bay window on the ground floor. Despite the tired and worn feel to the dwelling, Jon was surprised at how much land surrounded it, enclosed by low, wooden fencing, indicating it was all part of the ownership. Although he supposed that made sense, if this place had once been a farm.

It was fair to say that Danni's childhood home wasn't quite what Jon had been expecting, but then Danni had never really gone into any detail about it before.

The lack of upkeep, crossed with the clashing of the two different, but distinct, buildings standing out in otherwise open fields, gave a feeling of sad isolation.

And this is where Danni grew up.

This was her inheritance.

Up ahead, there was a small turning to the right that led

up to the property, and Jon carefully pulled the SUV into it. He winced as he heard the branches of the untended hedges scrape at the sides of his car, but he pressed on and took them up the long, dirt driveway, to the front of the house.

The building grew larger before them as they approached, and an odd, uneasy feeling washed over Jon.

He turned to Danni, who now looked petrified. 'You ready, hun?'

She took a breath and nodded, though her expression told a completely different story.

There were no other vehicles present, and no sign as yet of the solicitor they were due to meet. Jon thought about getting them all out of the car and inside of the house while they waited, but could feel Danni's apprehension radiate from her, and decided that staying in the car might help ease her tension.

Looking past the house to the back corner of what formed the rear garden, Jon spotted something he had not seen on the drive up: what appeared to be a few dilapidated, wooden outbuildings.

Jon guessed that Danni had inherited well over an acre of land. It may not be in the most desirable of areas, but the sell-on would bring the family a nice little injection of cash. They could probably make even more if they were prepared to fix the property up, though he doubted Danni would be willing to spend any more time—or money—here than they needed to.

To Jon's surprise, Danni opened the passenger door and got out of the car. The rest of the family then, too, disembarked. Leah once again helped Alex, who steadied himself on his crutches. A light hint of manure rolled in from the surrounding fields.

'Smells nice,' Alex said.

Danni let a sad smile spread across her lips. 'Yeah, that smell brings back memories.'

'It's in the middle of nowhere,' Leah said. 'You lived way out here?'

'I did.'

'So how did you meet up with friends?'

'I walked,' Danni said with a laugh.

They explored the perimeter a little, taking everything in. Jon followed Danni's lead, not wanting to push things too quickly. He watched her closely as she studied the area, the building, the details—he could practically see the memories replaying in her mind, just by the distant look on her face.

There was no paved area to the rear of the house as there was around the front and sides; the property's walls simply met with overgrown grass. It wasn't the most even of gardens, either, the ground beneath his feet feeling both hard and lumpy. Not the best surface for Alex to be walking on.

'You doing okay, Alex?' he asked, concerned about his son keeping his footing.

'Yeah,' Alex said, moving around confidently.

'Just be careful. It'd be easy to fall out here.'

'I'm fine, Dad,' he said. 'Mom, what were all these sheds used for?'

'Nothing much when I lived here,' Danni said. 'Just for storing junk. Not sure what they were used for before that, though.'

'They look old,' Alex said. 'Were they part of the original farm?'

'Maybe,' Danni replied, 'I'm not sure.'

'What kind of farm did it used to be?' Leah said, tiptoeing across the garden trying not to dirty her shoes.

'Just a normal farm,' Danni said. 'Cattle, crops, corn, and the like. Nothing special.'

'So why did it change?' Alex pressed. 'You know, why isn't it a farm anymore?'

Danni paused for a moment, as if choosing her words carefully. 'Well, there was a fire here quite a few years ago. The only thing that survived was that ugly mill,' she said, pointing to the cylindrical structure behind them. 'Apparently, all the other original buildings burned down.'

'So, did Grandpa build the new house?' Alex asked.

Danni turned to look at her son. 'What did you call him?'

'Grandpa,' Alex said.

Danni paused, again measuring her words. 'He wasn't your grandpa, Alex. You didn't know him, so there's no need to call him that.'

'But he is, technically—' the boy was going to go on and explain his logic, but Jon rested a hand on his shoulder, cutting him off.

'Just call him Arthur, Son.'

He looked more than a little confused, but shrugged and went along with it. 'Okay, did Arthur build this house?'

Danni shook her head and turned away. 'No,' she said, hugging herself as if to protect from the cold, 'he didn't. It was already built when we moved in.'

'Hasn't been very well looked after,' Leah said, peering in through the rear entrance, which was a fully glazed, sliding, double-door set.

'No,' Danni agreed. 'It never was. Not since my mom passed away.'

They all fell silent. Danni still stared off into the distance, and to Jon she looked like a lost and scared child. He went to her and wrapped his arms around her waist from behind, pulling her into him and kissing her on the back of her neck.

'It's going to be okay,' he whispered to her.

A humming noise from behind startled them all. It took Jon a moment to realise what it was; a car engine. He walked around the side of the house to see a black BMW, an older model, slowly crawl up the driveway.

'Solicitor is here,' he yelled, and his family joined him at the front of the property. Through the windshield, Jon could see the driver had a rotund face with bright red cheeks and messy red hair. Not the most professional-looking solicitor he had ever seen.

The rest of the family watched the car slowly approach as well, all except Alex, Jon noticed. The boy had his eyes firmly fixed on an upstairs window overlooking the front of the house.

'Hey,' Jon whispered, drawing his son's attention. 'You okay?'

'Yeah,' Alex said, giving his head a quick shake.

'What is it?' Jon asked, looking up to the window, but seeing nothing of interest.

Alex paused, studying the window again, then looked away. 'Nothing,' he finally said.

Jon was about to push it further, but the solicitor stopped the car and got out.

The unkempt man walked over to Jon and held out his hand.

'Hello,' he said, in a chirpy and high-pitched voice. 'The name is Winston Goldacre.'

4

'PLEASED TO MEET YOU ALL,' Winston Goldacre said after shaking their hands. 'Sorry for your loss, Mrs. Morgan,' he added, casting a mournful glance to Danni.

'Thank you,' she said, trying to hide the grimace she wanted to make as his plump, sweaty palm touched her skin. Part of her wanted to tell him not to feel bad about her father's death, that she certainly didn't, but she felt that would have come across as needlessly cold.

'When is the funeral?' he asked, though Danni got the feeling he wasn't asking out of genuine curiosity, but more an attempt at small talk.

'Tomorrow,' she said in reply.

'Very good,' Winston answered, running a meaty hand through the wispy remains of his red, unkempt hair, trying in vain to tame it. 'I take it you will be staying here until then?'

Danni nodded in response. 'Just long enough to get everything in order and put the house on the market, then we will be going home.'

'I see,' he said, and offered a smile. 'Not much around here to keep you anymore, I suppose?'

Again, Danni nodded. 'That is correct.'

'Well,' he said, clapping his hands together. 'We have a little bit of paperwork to get through, but nothing too oner- ous. Should we head inside and get on with it? I can then leave the keys with you and get out of your hair.'

'Sounds good,' Danni said.

But it didn't sound good. She had no desire to go inside the house. Just being on its grounds was almost too much to bear. The familiarity of everything was overwhelming. Echoes of a past that she thought, hoped, had been lost to the mists of time were now forcing their way back to the surface.

As they approached the front door, Danni took another glimpse at the mill. The place always scared her as a child, but there was one memory in particular that was vying for her attention. She remembered living here as a young girl, not long after her mother's death; her father dragged her out here in the rain. She had pleaded with him, but he simply would not listen, acting in unreasonable anger. She couldn't remember doing anything to cause this rage, but her punishment—he had decided—was to be locked in the mill for the night.

She remembered being thrown inside, and the thun- derous sound of the door slamming shut behind her. She heard the key turn in the lock, leaving her in complete dark- ness. No matter how much she kicked and begged, he would not release her. He just left her, alone and terrified. After that, all she could really remember was the fear—the rest seemed to be blocked out, just a dark void in her mind. The only clear memory after that was the next morning, when he opened the door to let her out. She didn't speak for three days after that night.

Growing up, she could never tell what it would take to cause her father to flip into an uncontrollable rage. It seemed so random. He could be distant and quiet one minute and a monster the next, with no warning of when the change was to come.

Being back here, facing these memories, was an overwhelming experience, and it was taking a lot for Danni to hold everything together. She knew this would only get worse when she finally stepped inside the house she'd run away from so many years ago. As if on cue, she felt Jon slip his large hand into her own and grip it tight. She turned to him and pulled a forced smile across her lips.

'You okay?' he asked quietly.

'I'll be fine,' she whispered so only he could hear. She didn't believe it, though, not deep down, not now that she was here. Facing your fears and laying to rest ghosts of the past might have seemed like a healthy idea, especially back in the safety of London, but now that they were here, it just felt too real.

Too immediate.

And she felt too vulnerable.

They stopped at the front door as Mr. Goldacre rummaged around in his pocket for the keys. As they waited, Danni noticed two large plant pots either side of the entrance. But whatever plants were inside had long since died, and the pot was now filled with dead leaves and swampy soil. Mr. Goldacre finally found they keys and, somewhat reluctantly, unlocked the door. He made a move to enter, but stopped, and moved aside.

'Sorry, where are my manners,' he said, and motioned for them to go ahead of him. 'After you.'

Danni also paused, instinctively, so Jon stepped forward instead and pushed open the door. Danni watched her husband, looking for his reaction, but there was barely any to speak of.

'Could do with a clean,' he simply said, and stepped inside. Danni realised that Leah and Alex were watching her, waiting for her to enter. She smiled at them, trying to hide her trepidation, to push it down and bury it before stepping inside herself. Jon was already a few steps ahead in the entrance hallway, inspecting his surroundings.

As Danni crossed the threshold, she felt the weight of the dingy, grimy house fall heavily onto her. It was almost tangible.

More memories flooded back, more feelings of unwelcome familiarity. The staircase, though dusty and now missing some spindles, was as she remembered it: made of old wood that always creaked with every other step. It led up to a first floor that seemed, even in the daytime, lost in shadows.

There was a doorway to the right of the hallway that she knew led into a large living room, and straight ahead was the door to the kitchen and dining area.

Jon poked his head into the living room, then kept walking towards the kitchen. Danni felt her children file in behind her, and heard the *click, click, click* of Alex's crutches finding purchase with the timber floor. The hallway felt oppressive, in no small part because of the low ceilings the house suffered from, and also because, other than what spilled in from the open front door, the narrow passageway was afforded no natural light.

Danni followed Jon's lead and looked into the living room as she passed. Some of the furniture had changed, though not necessarily for the better, as a lot of it looked second-hand and not in the best condition, but the basic layout was how she remembered it: a sofa lining the back wall, two large chairs—one close to the bay window—and a low coffee table being the centre piece of the room. There was still no T.V., and she also noticed that there were no pictures on the walls anymore, but the faded outlines of where they had once hung were still visible.

Seeing enough, she then joined Jon in the kitchen area. It had a large dining space adjacent, to the right, that contained the same dining room table she remembered from her childhood. It was a strong piece of furniture, made of fine oak—a gift from one of her mother's relatives. One of the few things the family owned that was worth anything.

She remembered hiding from her father under there once, as he yelled for her to show herself. She remembered his heavy footsteps stalking through the house before he found her...

The kitchen seemed bare, with only an old gas cooker, microwave, and toaster accompanying the old wooden kitchen units. Danni noted the lack of a washing machine, something they had never grown up with. An old mop stood isolated in the corner, the material at the bottom far too dirty to possibly clean anything.

Mr. Goldacre moved past them all and set his briefcase down on the dining room table. He unclipped it, pulled out a bundle of papers, and placed them down onto the table's surface.

'Shall we get started?' he asked, taking a seat.

'I guess so,' Jon said as he and Danni joined Mr. Goldacre at the table.

'How long will this take?' Leah asked.

'I'm hoping no more than half an hour,' Mr. Goldacre said.

'Can we have a look around the house, then?' Alex asked. 'It's not like there is anything else to do.'

'Can't you just play on your phones for a little while?' Danni asked.

'We can't,' Alex said, shaking his phone in his hand. 'The signal isn't very good here.'

'And there isn't any Wi-Fi,' Leah added. Danni sighed and looked to Jon.

'Fine,' he said. 'But be careful.'

'It's just a house, Dad,' Alex said.

'Yes, but we don't know what condition it's in. So, like I said, be careful.'

'We will,' Leah said. 'Come on, Alex, let's see if we inherited anything cool.'

She walked out of the room and Alex followed.

Click, click, click.

Danni gave Jon a worried look.

'They'll be fine,' he said. 'And they're right, you know. It is just a house.'

But would they be fine? As a parent, Danni naturally worried about her children most of the time, but being here, in this state of mind, only made things worse. She just wanted to hold them close and never let them go. Especially Alex, who had enough to deal with in life as it was. If anything were to happen to them—any of them, including Jon—she didn't know what she would do.

Mr. Goldacre interrupted them with a theatrical cough. 'If we can get down to business,' he said, and started quickly flicking through the paperwork.

Danni and Jon shared a confused look. To Danni, he seemed genuinely nervous. Though she couldn't be sure, she had a feeling he was anxious just being in this house.

What's got you so spooked, buddy?

ALEX FOLLOWED his sister up the stairs, hearing them creak under his weight. Leah kept glancing back over her shoulder to check on him, which was something he was used to. But he didn't need it—he'd learned to cope with what life had thrown at him, though he would never complain about his family looking out for each other.

They reached the top and looked around. The stairs hugged the far-left gable wall of the building, and as they got to the top they saw that the landing ran off to the right, revealing a darkened corridor lined with four doors. Directly above them on the landing, Alex saw an attic hatch, framed in the ceiling. It was chipped and cracked and had a hole in one corner, letting the absolute darkness from the void behind creep out.

The walls seemed like they had once been painted white, or magnolia, but the colour had been tainted to a kind of dirty yellow, and they were lightly streaked with what looked like dust or dirt. Squinting, Alex thought he could even see faded handprints on the walls as well.

'Arthur wasn't big on cleaning, huh?' he said.

'Tell me about it,' Leah replied. 'Do you think we should call him grandpa?'

Alex shrugged. 'Not if Mom doesn't want us to. I guess she's right, we didn't know him at all, so he doesn't really feel like a grandpa.'

'Yeah,' she said, nodding. 'I know what you mean.'

They progressed down the corridor, the bare floorboards creaking beneath them as they went. All the doors off the hallway were closed, and the first one they arrived at was missing a handle. Leah nudged it with her foot, and it slowly swung open, revealing a large bedroom—one without much furniture. The only thing of any note was the long window on the far wall. More handprints could be seen against the faded paint, in seemingly random patterns.

'Guest room?' Leah asked.

'I think so,' Alex said. He moved past Leah into the room while she leaned against the door frame, obviously preferring not to enter.

'Feels creepy,' she said.

'Yeah,' Alex agreed, then coughed. The whole house, but particularly the first floor, seemed to be filled with floating dust that stuck to the back of his throat. He walked to the middle of the room, but there was nothing of interest. He felt a chill run up his spine. 'Creepy,' he echoed, then turned to face his sister.

That's when he saw the old woman standing directly behind Leah.

Her blackened mouth was pulled into a horrible smile.

Alex screamed.

5

—————

DANNI WAS up out of her chair before the sound of her child's frightened screams had finished reverberating around the house. Jon followed, but struggled to keep pace as Danni bounded up the stairs.

'What is it?' she yelled, taking the steps two at a time. 'Alex? Leah?'

She ran to the right, into the corridor, and saw that only one of the doors was open. She ran into that room, thinking only of getting to her children, and saw Leah kneeling in front of Alex with her hand on his shoulder. He looked white and shaken.

'What is it?' Danni asked, running to Alex's side.

'I don't know,' Leah said, looking concerned. 'He just freaked out. Are you okay?' she asked him.

Alex was looking past them all, into the corridor. Danni turned to follow his gaze, but saw nothing out of the ordinary, only Jon arriving to the room.

'Alex,' she said, turning his head so he looked directly at her. 'What is it, honey?'

'I...' he said, then trailed off. She saw it in his face, he was struggling with something. 'Nothing,' he said eventually. 'I thought I saw something.'

'What did you see?' Danni asked, trying to coax it out of him, but he just shook his head.

'Nothing,' he said, more firmly this time, visibly taking charge of his nerves. He straightened himself up and took a deep breath. 'It must have been a shadow or something. Sorry, I'm probably a little jumpy.'

Danni was conflicted. She was relieved that everything was okay, of course, as it gave her heart—which was physically trying to beat through her chest—a chance to calm down. But on the other hand, she felt like Alex was holding something back from her, and she knew him well enough to realise that, even though something had scared him, he wouldn't let on as to what it was. He seemed more than a little embarrassed at the whole thing, and his pride had now kicked in, overriding whatever fear had once come over him.

'You sure you're okay, Son?' Jon asked, setting a hand gently on his shoulder. Alex nodded.

'I'm fine,' Alex said, then Danni noticed his attention turn to the door again. She spun her head, half expecting to see what had frightened him so, but instead made out the head of Mr. Goldacre peeking around the frame.

'Everything okay?' he asked.

'Yeah,' Jon answered. 'Nothing to worry about.'

'Good,' the solicitor replied, but Danni once again detected that nervousness, that apprehension, on his face. 'Shall we keep going?'

~

LEAH HAD SUGGESTED THAT, instead of exploring the first

floor any further, it might be a good idea to go outside and walk the grounds while Mom and Dad finished off with Mr. Goldacre. Alex had no doubt that his sister had suggested this purely for his benefit, and he loved her for it. He agreed without hesitation.

The two siblings headed outside, and their parents returned to the dining room to get on with business—though Mom didn't seem too eager to leave them alone. Alex took in a deep breath of late afternoon air and looked to the sun, which was drawing near to the horizon.

Being outside felt better. It was less oppressive than being in the house, less overwhelming. Alex wasn't sure how else to describe it, but everything in there just felt... off. But he chalked that up to nerves, frazzled by his recent fright. One, he convinced himself, that had been brought on by nothing but his imagination.

Surely the creepy old woman he had seen earlier couldn't have been real?

After the fright, he had wanted to tell his mother everything. When she had burst into that room to check on him he had almost started to cry, and was on the cusp of telling her just what he had seen. All in the hope that she could make it better for him.

But he knew that was childish.

Seeing his father arrive just after gave him steel. He wouldn't let something so stupid, so childish, make his dad disappointed in him.

Like his father, science was Alex's belief system. What he had seen was a trick of the mind, nothing more, triggered by tiredness, or stress, or some other unknown cause.

It had to be.

But at the time he had believed, without question, without any doubt, that there was someone, *something*, standing directly behind his sister. Looming over her shoulder.

Looking at him.

While the thing had seemed shrouded in unnatural shadow, he could clearly see it was a woman. A really, really old woman, with ashen skin pulled tight over the skull beneath. He could still see her blackened smile and wide, staring eyes.

It was the eyes that had really scared him. The way they seemed to bore into him with a manic gaze.

In that moment, in that instant, there had been no question in his mind that someone was there. But now, in the clear light of the evening, with the air on his face, reality once again took hold.

Thankfully.

It wasn't real. He had just spooked himself, even though he thought he was above all of that kind of nonsense.

Obviously not.

Almost as bad as the fright he had given himself was the panic he'd seen on his mother's face when she entered the room and set eyes upon him. He hated the fact that she worried about him so. Actually, no, that wasn't right. He hated the fact that he was the cause of her worry. Everyone in the family looked out for him, it was natural, and he actually liked it, but when that turned into worry and fear—when he and his condition caused people to fret and panic—that didn't sit well with him. It made him feel like a burden. And that was exactly how he had felt when he saw that look of fear etched on his mother's face.

Over something so stupid.

Stupid, stupid, stupid.

Alex continued ambling around the rear garden, looking out over the fields beyond. He had to admit, despite the fact

that the house wasn't to his liking, the immediate surroundings were very picturesque and peaceful. Part of him could
see the appeal of living somewhere like this, though relocating here wasn't something he hoped his parents would
ever consider. He liked it too much back home.

Growing bored, he turned back towards his sister to ask
how much longer she thought this would take, and saw she
was looking to an upstairs window, squinting. He also
noticed that she had her right hand over her chest, and was
holding her breath. Her mouth was ever so slightly agape.

'Everything okay?' he asked, causing her to jump a little.
She spun her head to face him, and eventually nodded.

'Yeah, fine,' she said.

'What is it?'

'Nothing,' she replied, a little too quickly.

'You're not seeing things as well, are you?' He tried to
laugh when he said it, but it came out forced.

'Don't be stupid,' Leah answered with a painstakingly
fake laugh of her own. 'Come on, they should be finished
soon, and the sun is starting to set. Let's go back inside.'

Alex nodded in agreement and followed her lead. He
was eager to press her on the issue, but, knowing how he felt
after his own scare, decided against it.

As he walked, he glanced up at the window Leah had
been staring at, slightly apprehensive about what he
would find.

He saw nothing.

∾

'AND THAT SHOULD BE EVERYTHING,' Mr. Goldacre said as he
bundled together his papers and slotted them into a binder.
Danni and Jon had been left with copies of the paperwork,

and now Danni officially owned the house. Jon knew she would want it on the market as quickly as possible, but that was something they could deal with when they got back home.

First and foremost, his wife had to get through the funeral tomorrow—the funeral of a father she hadn't seen in half her lifetime—and he wasn't sure how she would cope with that.

They had also agreed to stay in the house while they were here, which saved on finding and booking accommodation. Danni hadn't been keen on it, but Jon had pushed the idea, gently but firmly, believing it would help with any healing she had to go through whilst back here.

Jon had suffered difficulties in his youth as well—not to the extent that Danni had, but he found that facing up to the challenges and confronting them head-on was the only way to truly overcome them. He knew just how strong Danni was, stronger than she ever gave herself credit for. When she stopped overthinking things and just acted from the heart, she was fearless. A lioness.

He knew she was capable of getting through this.

He'd seen her show that strength before.

Many years ago, when Alex was only two years old, he had fallen and hurt himself. If Jon was completely honest, he had panicked and frozen, but Danni had reacted on instinct, getting Alex to the emergency room in a heartbeat. When the nurse behind the counter—an impatient, bordering on uncaring old woman—had said it may be a little while before Alex could be seen, Danni had slammed her hand onto the counter and stated, in a scarily calm way, that he would be seen immediately. It wasn't a request, not even a demand, just how things were going to be, and there was no possibility of any deviation from that course of action. The nurse had tried to argue back, but Danni had unloaded on her. There had been no foul language, no threats of any kind, she had just overpowered the old woman by sheer force of will and strength of character alone. The woman, obviously used to dishing out the orders and not taking them, had fallen in line.

And Alex had been seen immediately.

The problem now was that Danni had ample time to overthink things. She was clearly dealing with memories of what had happened, and they were already weighing her down.

But she could do this. He knew she could.

Mr. Goldacre put away his things and got to his feet, shaking both of their hands. 'We have your details, should we need anything further,' he said, walking to the entrance hallway just as Alex and Leah entered. He smiled at them and squeezed past without stopping, which Jon found odd. The man was certainly in a rush.

'If we are going to put this on the market straight away,' Jon said, 'would it be best to do it with a local estate agent?'

'I would say so,' Mr. Goldacre said, not slowing as he walked to his car. Jon found himself following quickly, with Danni and the kids in tow, just to keep the conversation going. 'There are a few in town. I would always recommend Harrison's. They're a family-run business and should look after you,' Mr. Goldacre said.

He pulled open the door of his car and jumped in, throwing his briefcase into the passenger seat. Jon looked to the back, and saw it was cluttered with loose papers, food wrappers, folders, and other junk.

'Thanks,' Jon said. 'Appreciate the help with everything. Will you be at the funeral tomorrow?'

'Oh no,' Goldacre said, quickly, then caught himself. 'I'm

very busy, and we tend not to overstep our bounds attending things like that. We see them as personal affairs. People don't want stuffy old solicitors getting in the way of their mourning.'

'Okay,' Jon said. 'If we have any questions, I assume we are okay to call you?'

'Of course,' he said, pulling the car door shut and starting the engine. He rolled down the window. 'Anything you need, just call.' He pulled a smile across his face, but Jon could sense his agitation, like the conversation was holding him up. 'You have my card.'

'I do,' Jon said.

'Then take care,' Mr. Goldacre said, before looking past him to the house. The man's smile fell and he was silent for a moment, as if caught in a trance, or a memory. 'Good luck with everything,' he eventually said. 'It was nice meeting you all, sorry it wasn't under better circumstances. Take care.'

He waved and pulled the car forward, whizzing down to the main road, kicking up dust and dirt as he went.

'Well,' Leah said, 'he was a little odd.'

6

————

THE FAMILY SPENT the rest of the day getting as settled into the house as they could. Danni had brought supplies, spare sheets, and even an inflatable air bed with them, should they be needed. The house had three bedrooms: two spare ones and the master. That one had belonged to her father—and there was no way any of them would sleep in there—so she and Jon claimed one of the spare rooms and gave the children the other. The beds were dusty and unkempt, so she had insisted on replacing the sheets with their own, a job that hadn't taken them long. But there was only a double bed in each room, so Alex wanted to use the inflatable bed, which Danni could understand. What fourteen-year-old boy would want to share a bed with his sister?

Leah had offered, even insisted, that she use the inflatable, but Alex had won out, not taking no for an answer. He was being chivalrous, Danni knew, and it made her even more proud of the boy, if that was possible.

After getting the house in some kind of order, the next item on the list was to organise the food. They didn't even bother to check the cupboards, or attempt to cook, and Jon had taken his phone outside—the only place to get a signal —to search for local takeaways in the area. They had all decided on pizza, and, when he found an outlet that suited, he ordered it in.

There wasn't much to do in the house with no television or internet, and Danni tried to remember what life was like without so many gadgets taking up all of their attention. Thankfully, they had all come prepared, each with an e-reader or tablet, with entertainment pre-loaded.

In the living room, Alex and Leah took to the sofa, Alex with his Kindle, and Leah watching something on her tablet with her headphones plugged in. Jon led Danni to the chair by the window, which was really only big enough for one, and pulled her into it with him. She giggled as he let her fall into his lap, and they spent the time cuddling while waiting for their food. It was exactly what she needed right now. Sometimes, she thought her husband just might be a mind reader.

The pizza arrived and, truth be told, wasn't great. It was serviceable, however, and by the end of the meal at least they all had full bellies. The food helped Danni feel a touch more human, though it only exacerbated her exhaustion. She felt like she could drop into a deep sleep at the snap of a finger.

Maybe that wasn't such a bad thing.

They had eaten at the dining room table, all quiet except for the slurps and smacks of chewing mouths. Once done, they moved back into the living room, and Leah spoke up.

'I'm going for a shower. I feel grubby.'

'Is there hot water?' Danni asked.

'I got the heating going a little earlier,' Jon said. 'Seems to be working, so we should be okay for showers.'

It wasn't until Jon mentioned it that Danni realised the room had started feeling a little warmer.

'Okay,' Danni said, 'but be quick.' She had no idea why she'd said it, or why such a warning was necessary. They were alone in this house and, despite how much Danni hated being here, they weren't in any danger.

So why couldn't she shake the feeling that just the opposite was true?

Leah left to take her shower and Danni heard her padding around upstairs, getting her toiletries together.

'Do you want to shower after Leah?' she asked Alex.

'I'll just wait until the morning,' he said.

'Okay,' Danni said, pausing to think how to broach the next part. 'When you do go, just remember that the bathroom isn't set up like ours back home. It doesn't have any handrails or anything like that. Might be better if—'

'You aren't washing me, Mom,' he said, cutting her off. 'I'll manage. I'm capable of showering by myself.'

'I know you are, hun,' Danni said. 'And at home, I wouldn't mind, but this bathroom is old and—'

'No,' he said, matter-of-factly, again cutting her off. 'I'll be fine, Mom. If I need you, or get stuck, I'll shout.'

'Hun...'

'Mom,' Alex said. He was smiling, but Danni knew he was being as assertive as he could be. 'I'm doing it on my own. I'll be fine.'

Danni wanted to press the issue, but knew she would get nowhere. Alex's pride was front and centre again, and evidently her approach had failed. Maybe it was something she should broach again in the morning. She heard the faint sound of the shower come on from the floor above.

'Fine,' she said, and rose to her feet. She walked over to her son and playfully tussled his hair.

'Mom,' he said to her, looking up from his e-reader. 'I'm sorry if I freaked you out earlier.'

'What do you mean?' Danni asked.

'You know, upstairs. I'm sorry about that.'

'Oh,' Danni said. 'It's okay.'

'I'm not sure what happened to you here, but I get the impression that being back isn't easy for you. And I know you're going to be sad, especially tomorrow, so I don't want to make things any worse for you.'

Danni smiled, feeling her heart twinge. She hadn't told her children about her past, not yet—they were too young for that and didn't need to know. Whenever they'd asked about her parents, she had just told them that her mother had died many years ago, and she didn't speak with her father. They sometimes pressed the issue, and she told them he just wasn't a nice person. They soon got the message: that it wasn't a topic to be pushed. 'Honestly, Alex, it's fine. You don't need to be sorry.'

'Well, I am. I don't want to make you feel bad. I never want that. And I kind of feel like I did.'

Danni bent down and hugged Alex tight.

'I appreciate that,' she said. 'It's very sweet of you to say. But I'm made of tough stuff. I'm fine. Honestly.'

'Good,' he said, and hugged her back. It was rare Danni ever got to hug him like this anymore. He was becoming a young man, and as such, hugs from Mom were seen as less and less cool, and more and more embarrassing. She savoured the moment and wanted it to last as long as it could, feeling the first pangs of happiness she'd had since her arrival in this town.

Before she could enjoy it any further, she heard Leah's terrified screams from above.

THE WATER in the shower was warm, thankfully.

Leah had half expected it to be freezing. Or, worse, for the old showerhead to kick out dull, dirty water. To her surprise, though, the water looked clear, and the pressure was strong.

It felt good.

The bathroom itself was small for a house this size. The shower was an over-bath type, with fully tiled walls to one end of the bath, complete with a shower screen. The tiles were faintly streaked with dirt, and the glass folding screen had black mould growing at its corners. The bath itself wasn't the cleanest, either, and Leah had to force herself to get in. It was worth it, though, as she could feel the hot water blast away some of her aches and pains from a long day's travel. She stood motionless, letting the water hit the back of her neck and cascade down her. Steam soon filled the room.

Remembering her mother's instructions not to stay up here too long, Leah began to wash, pouring shampoo onto her scalp and massaging it in.

Leah didn't like this house and guessed that none of the family did, either. It was old, uncared for, not very homely, and gave off an ominous vibe. A dirty and withering place.

And it absolutely creeped her out.

And not just because of the state it was in, either. After she had taken Alex outside earlier, after his scare, a strong and distinct feeling had crept over her. A feeling like she was being watched.

It was like nothing she had ever felt before. The hairs on the back of her arms and neck had stood to attention, and she'd instinctively turned to look up to a first-floor window.

There was dirty netting to the inside, with curtains framing it, so her view wasn't clear, but Leah was almost certain she had seen something: the shadowy outline of a person standing just behind the netting, looking out at them.

Perfectly still and unmoving.

At first she thought she was mistaken, but the more she looked, the more she was sure.

Then Alex had asked if she was okay, drawing her attention, and when she had looked back, everything had seemed normal.

Whatever she had seen, or thought she had seen, was gone.

Of course, she soon realised there never had been anything there at all. No shadowy figure watching over them. But at the time, it had seemed so real.

And ominous.

Just thinking about it now caused a sensation of unease to course through her, starting at the small of her back and working its way up to her shoulders, making the warm water actually feel cold.

Leah was creeping herself out, she knew that—her mind

was getting carried away with itself. It was stupid, but even so, she decided she'd been up here alone long enough. She let the suds rinse from her hair and opened her eyes.

Something was wrong.

Through the steamed glass of the shower screen, she could see the door to the bathroom. It was open a little.

But she was certain she had closed it when entering the room.

Hadn't she?

Obviously not. She ran a hand down the screen, wiping away some of the steam in order to see more clearly. It was definitely open, just a crack, and there was something else too.

It took a moment for it to register, for her brain to make sense of what she was seeing. If indeed such a thing could be made sense of.

The pale skin of a torso, a male torso.

She held her breath and looked up farther, to the top of the door.

She saw the face.

Looking at her.

Its eyes were wide and full of hateful lust. Its mouth was agape, dropping unnaturally low, almost elongated.

And its tongue lolled loosely, like that of a dog.

She heard it moan—a pained sound, but one that belied a sinister urge.

Bestial.

Carnal.

Watching her as she showered.

A loud, instinctive scream erupted from her.

～

ONCE AGAIN, Danni found herself acting on impulse, and she raced up the stairs to help one of her children who, yet again, seemed to be in need. The same feeling of panic and rush of adrenaline shot through her. Again, she was the first to react, the quickest, with Jon running behind her.

Leah continued to scream.

It was different from when she had heard Alex yell earlier. He had screamed once, but this sound was continuous, and to Danni that meant danger.

Something was happening.

It's this fucking house, she said to herself. *We shouldn't be here. It was a stupid fucking idea, and I should have left the old fucker to rot in here alone.*

Danni barrelled headlong into the first-floor corridor and saw the door to the bathroom slightly ajar, steam pouring out of the room. She kicked the door open and launched herself inside, braced for something.

Anything.

Leah was curled up on the floor of the bathtub.

She was huddled into a foetal position, and was screaming incessantly. Without thinking, Danni ran to her and took hold of her, pulling her up into a crouched hug. The water still sprayed from the shower, soaking Danni, but she barely noticed.

'What is it?' she asked, breathless, as Jon ran in behind her.

Leah didn't answer, she just continued to cry. Jon turned off the shower and looked around, panicked and confused.

'What happened, Leah?' Danni asked again, more firmly this time. She saw that her daughter, whilst scared, appeared physically unharmed. However, that didn't mean any potential danger had passed, and she needed to know what had frightened her daughter so. She needed to know what to do to protect her.

'Someone was outside of the door,' Leah said softly, her voice not much more than a whisper.

'What?' Jon asked, urgency and disbelief in his voice. He dashed to the corridor outside, and Danni heard him then run from room to room, searching.

'Who was it?' Danni asked. She grabbed the towel and draped it over her daughter to help warm her trembling body.

'I don't know,' she said. The young adult that Leah was growing into was momentarily gone, replaced with a frightened child. 'But he was just standing there, watching me.'

'Mom!' came a concerned voice. It was Alex, shouting up from the bottom stairs. Danni could hear him making his way up. 'Is everything okay? Is Leah all right?'

'She's fine, hun,' Danni called back, rubbing Leah's arms and shoulders in an effort to stop the shaking. 'Everything is okay. But stay down there.'

But it wasn't okay, was it? Nothing felt okay. Nothing about this seemed right.

Something was very off.

She heard Alex work his way up the stairs anyway, and felt a split second of anger, annoyed that he had seen fit to ignore her.

Jon re-entered the room.

'There's no one here,' he said. 'I've checked everywhere.'

'I saw somebody, I swear,' Leah said. 'Someone was standing right there.' She pointed to the space just outside the doorway, just behind Jon. A space Alex filled as he stepped into view. He looked worried, too, which was only natural, Danni supposed, considering the horrible screams that had been coming from Leah only moments ago.

Then Danni remembered that only a little while earlier, it had been Alex who had been the frightened one, the one who had been screaming.

Because of something—he said—he *thought* he saw.

Something was definitely wrong with this place.

Danni felt it.

'There's no one here, sweetie,' Jon said. 'I've checked everywhere.'

'But I saw someone,' she said as tears continued to run down her face. 'I'm not making it up.'

'Are you sure?' Jon asked, trying to sound as gentle as possible, but he couldn't hide the skepticism in his voice. Leah buried her face into the towel, pulling it up around her shoulders, and continued to sob.

'I know what I saw, Dad,' she said, not bothering to hide the anger in her voice.

Danni looked up to Jon. He shook his head and shrugged his shoulders. The message was clear: as much as he loved his daughter, he didn't believe her. If someone had been up here, Jon would have found them. The place wasn't that big, and there weren't that many places to hide. No one had passed them coming down the stairs.

Despite all of that, and the logic that would indicate Jon was right, Danni knew her daughter.

And she believed her.

'Come on, honey,' Danni said, coaxing Leah up to a standing position. 'Let's get you dried and dressed. Then we'll all go downstairs. I'll make us a warm drink and we can talk about it.'

Leah raised her red eyes to meet Danni's. She looked deathly afraid. When she spoke, it was a whisper.

'We aren't alone here.'

8

JON AND ALEX headed downstairs and left Danni to help Leah compose herself. Jon walked in front of Alex as they descended, but kept turning his head to watch his son as the boy navigated the old stairs. They then moved into the living room where Alex took a seat. Jon noticed Alex rub his wrists, clearly sore from the strain of the plastic wrist-supports attached to the aluminium crutches.

'What do you think happened, Dad?' Alex asked, and Jon could see the worry in his face.

'Nothing,' Jon said, not wanting Alex to fall foul of any kind of hysteria. Jon was quite sure there was no one in the house with them, and that Leah's episode had been brought on by something else. Maybe the stress of the situation was filtering down to the children in ways he hadn't envisioned. Alex, too, had experienced an incident of his own, but thankfully was be able to rationalise it. He wanted that to continue. 'I think with everything that's going on, and the fact we're in a new place, one that's pretty creepy, imaginations are running away with themselves. But I promise you, Son, there is nothing to worry about here.'

Alex nodded and smiled. 'Okay,' he said.

'And we need to be strong for your mother and sister,' Jon went on. 'We need to make sure we don't let little things spook us, you understand what I'm saying? If we make a big deal over things that turn out to be nothing, we aren't helping anyone.'

'I understand,' Alex said, with another nod.

Jon smiled and patted his son's shoulder. 'I knew you would,' he said.

Soon, Danni and Leah returned to the living room and, as promised, Danni fixed them all hot drinks. She then tried to talk to Leah a little more, to pry a little more information from her, but Leah closed up. The girl just sat on the sofa next to her mother and brother, her knees pulled up to her chest. She took tentative sips from her hot chocolate, but remained silent. She had a glazed look in her eyes and was staring off into nothing.

It looked to Jon like she was suffering from a mild case of shock, so he knew something had genuinely spooked her. But, at the same time, he had checked everywhere he could, and had found nothing. When Leah had first told them someone was standing outside of the bathroom door watching her shower, he had felt a chill run down his spine. Could it be that someone was here in the house with them? In short order, that chill had turned to white hot fury, and he had set off to try to find whoever was there with the intent, he realised only now, to hurt them.

That feeling had soon subsided. He'd searched everywhere he could think of and had come up empty handed. It was then he'd realised that, more likely, Leah hadn't seen what she thought she had. Not to say she was lying—Jon knew his daughter better than that—but that she had been genuinely mistaken.

The shock she was now in, he reasoned, was either her mind's way of dealing with what it thought it saw, or, perhaps, it was a way for her to deal with the realisation that she was wrong and had scared everyone for nothing. Maybe she was dealing with the embarrassment of it all, which Jon could understand. The same thing had happened to Alex earlier, and perhaps that had—in part—fuelled Leah's subconscious, twisting the most mundane thing into something it was not.

'How about we all sleep together in here tonight?' Danni asked. Jon cast her a confused look.

'Is there space?' he asked.

'Might be a little snug,' Danni replied, 'but we can make it work. It'll be nice, all of us in the room together. Like a little sleepover.' She leaned in to Leah. 'That sound good with you?'

Leah nodded and took another sip from her drink. Jon understood what Danni was trying to do; if they were all in the same room together, Leah might feel more comfortable, though he didn't like it. He didn't want to wrap her up like that. She was strong, they all were, and the best way for Leah to pull through this was to return to normality. At least, as much as their present situation would allow. Staying in the same room with her parents, to Jon, was like letting a child sleep with the light on after a nightmare. It didn't really help.

It just reinforced that it was okay to be scared over nothing, and to let others come and fix everything.

'I'm not sure that is needed,' Jon said, and Danni shot him a scowl. 'I've looked everywhere, there's no one here. We'll be fine. Besides, Alex is in there with her.'

'I just thought—' Danni started to say, but Leah cut her off.

'It'll be fine,' Leah said quietly. She was looking up to Jon, and he saw that her cheeks had flushed a little. So she was embarrassed. He felt bad for making her feel that way, but knew that everyone huddling together down here, all scared of every shadow, was not helping anyone.

'Okay,' he said. 'Tell you what, to put everyone's minds to rest I'll go and search the house again. I'll check everywhere.'

Leah nodded and looked back to her drink, gently swirling it in the mug. Jon looked over to Danni and saw that his wife looked furious.

Again, he felt bad for adding to her worries this weekend, but by morning this would all be behind them, with more important things to concentrate on.

'Want me to come with you, Dad?' Alex asked.

'Thanks, buddy, but I'll be fine. You stay here with your mother and sister.'

Alex nodded, and Jon left the room to head upstairs. When he reached the top, he stood on the landing, looking to his right down the length of the dark corridor. He flicked on the light and then went room to room. First, to one of the spare bedrooms, then to the bathroom, which was still steamed up, then on to the master bedroom, Arthur's old room, and finishing with the last spare bedroom.

Nothing.

He came back to the landing, ready to make his descent, when a sound from behind alerted him. He turned and looked up, toward the attic hatch. Whatever the noise was, it didn't repeat itself. He couldn't place it, somewhere between a whisper and a gust of wind. Perhaps the roof was patchy and wind was spilling in from outside. He noticed that one corner of the attic hatch had a hole in it, and he could see the darkness behind.

He shook his head, not letting himself fall into the same trap Leah had earlier. It was an old house, and one that had quite an oppressive atmosphere, and a man had died here only days ago, so it was natural they would be unnerved.

Jon turned back to face the stairs.

The lights suddenly flickered.

Only briefly, but enough to stop him in his tracks. He paused, waiting for something else, half-expecting the lights to blink out completely.

Great, he thought to himself. *The lights going out in the house is just what I need right now.*

That would send his family into a complete panic.

And that's when he heard it; an exhale, directly behind him. He felt cold breath roll over the back of his neck.

He froze.

Impossible.

He didn't have time to turn around before a forceful push launched him down the stairs.

THE THUNDEROUS SOUND of something heavy crashing down the stairs caused Danni to jump. Leah jolted as well and pressed herself against her mother. The sound continued until whatever it was had settled at the bottom of the stairs.

Jon.

Danni pulled herself free of Leah, feeling like every time things had calmed down and were quiet, something else happened that forced her into action and raised her adrenaline again. She ran into the entrance hallway, hoping that maybe Jon had just dropped something down the stairs. She had no idea what that could be, but anything was better than what she pictured finding.

She brought her hands to her mouth and drew in a sharp intake of breath as she saw him.

Her worst fears were confirmed.

John lay crumpled at the bottom of the stairs, face down, with one arm behind his back and one leg resting on the bottom stair. He was motionless.

'Jon!' Danni yelled and ran to him.

'Dad!' she heard Alex scream from behind.

She shook her husband, careful not to be too firm in her movements, not knowing what injuries he may have suffered. 'Jon,' she said again, frantic. 'Are you okay? Please be okay?'

He moaned.

It was a pained, groggy sound, but one she was intensely glad to hear. It meant the worst had been avoided.

He was alive.

'Honey, are you okay? Can you move?'

Slowly, his arms began to untangle themselves, and he tried to roll over. Danni helped him do so, but made sure the movement was slow. She then helped him straighten out and settle onto his back.

'He's bleeding,' Alex pointed out.

Danni looked up to him as he spoke and saw Leah standing behind her brother with the same look of terror on her face that she'd seen only an hour or so before. Danni looked back down to Jon and saw blood smeared below his nose and over his mouth. It had also pooled on the bare wooden floor where his face had been resting.

Fuck! So much blood!

She searched for injury as his eyes fluttered open. She couldn't find any cuts or bruises on his mouth, and as he opened his lips she saw his teeth and gums were fine as well.

However, blood was spilling freely from his nose, though the appendage didn't look bent or disfigured.

He let out another, longer groan.

'Jesus,' he said, then focused his eyes on Danni.

'Are you okay?' she asked.

Please be okay, please be okay, please be okay.

'I think so,' he eventually said.

'Are you hurt?'

'My face feels sore.'

'Can you move?'

He winced and began to push himself upright into a sitting position. Blood ran down onto his top.

'I don't think anything is broken,' he said, forcing a pained smile that Danni knew was meant to reassure her. A nice gesture, but a futile one.

'Leah, Alex,' she said, turning to her children, 'one of you go and get some towels from the kitchen.'

Leah hesitated, but Alex carefully made his way through.

Danni turned back to Jon. 'What happened?'

He took his time answering, as if measuring his response. 'I lost my footing,' he said, 'and fell.'

Jon brought a hand to his face and pressed the back of it beneath his nose. He pulled it away and saw it was streaked with blood.

'Damn it,' he said.

'Anything else? Is anything broken?'

'I don't think so.' With Danni's help, Jon eased himself up to unsteady feet, resting one arm over her shoulder. He put his other hand on the stair banister for support. 'I think I bounced pretty good on the way down.'

Click, click, click.

Alex returned with a towel in hand. A drying cloth,

rather than a paper towel, but it would have to do. The blood would wash out, or they would throw it away. Right now, that didn't matter. He handed it to his mother who gently dabbed it around Jon's nose. Jon winced and pulled back.

'Sorry,' she said, handing the towel to him. 'Tilt your head back and press this to your nose to try to stop the bleeding.' He did as instructed, still using Danni for balance.

'Are you okay, Dad?' Alex asked.

'I'm fine, buddy,' Jon said, his voice muffled by the cloth.

'Come and sit down,' Danni said. 'I'll call a doctor, or an ambulance or something.'

'No need,' Jon said as Danni led him back through to the living room.

'There's every need,' she told him. 'You just fell down the stairs. You might have broken something.'

'I haven't,' he replied. 'It hurt, but there's no serious damage done. I may end up with a swollen nose, but that will be about it.'

Danni helped him onto the sofa. To her, he still looked a little dazed, but he seemed to be coming round. Danni allowed herself to feel a little more relieved and tried to calm her heart rate.

First Alex, then Leah, now Jon.

'Some trip,' she said. 'I'll be glad when we are back home and away from all this. We shouldn't have come.'

She rubbed her husband's free hand as he continued to dab at his nose. The bleeding seemed to be easing now, but his shirt was ruined.

'It's fine,' Jon said. 'Just a little run of bad luck. Nothing to worry about.'

It may have been her imagination, but Jon's normal, self-assured tone was gone.

It was as if he didn't really believe it himself.

9

LEAH DIDN'T SLEEP that night.

Her father's fall had shocked her. After seeing him laid out at the bottom of the stars, like a broken doll, she'd been sure the man she'd seen watching her in the shower had caused it. Her father had insisted, however, that he'd simply tripped. The only thing they had to be scared of, he had maintained, was their own clumsiness.

Shortly after, he'd suggested they all turn in for the night. Leah's mother seemed as reluctant as Leah to do so, but they both went along with the idea. Leah almost asked if she could sleep in her parents' room, like she had done as a child, but the shame of such a question had stopped her.

Lying in the old bed, with Alex on the inflatable mattress on the floor, Leah could hear his soft breathing grow into light snores. For some reason, knowing her brother was now asleep only served to further her unease. It was like she was alone in the room now, and whatever things lurked in the shadows would target her, and only her.

Such as that unnaturally tall, pale man. She pictured

him lunging forward from the darkness, arms outstretched, with that look of raw hunger and want in his eyes...

Enough!

Leah chastised herself for letting her imagination get out of control like that. But then again, was it *just* her imagination? She knew one thing for certain: she hadn't imagined that man watching her in the shower. Even if her father had searched the house and come up empty, it didn't change the fact that someone was there.

But if he had been there, then where was he now? Her father thought the fact they couldn't find him was proof he had never been here in the first place, but what if he'd just evaded detection?

What if he was still here, right now?

The thought of him skulking about in the shadows—as they all slept—caused Leah to shudder and pull the blankets a little farther up to her chin.

And worse, what if it wasn't even a man at all?

As implausible as it sounded, she wasn't ready to dismiss the notion that he, or it, could be something else. Before tonight, Leah always thought she was pragmatic, like the rest of her family, and she always believed that things that went bump in the night were nothing but stories.

Make-believe.

There were no such things as ghosts, demons, or monsters. She had always been certain of that, as she was taught. Their father pressed upon them that if these things were real, there would be evidence, and in the many, many years of sightings and experiences, there had been no tangible evidence to speak of.

That had always made perfect sense to her.

And now... she couldn't be sure of that anymore. After seeing what she had, it certainty called everything into question. After all, what more evidence did she need than what her own eyes provided for her?

Again, she tried to pull her thoughts away from the horrible experience, away from what she had seen. She tried to forget the man and his elongated body, the lolling mouth and flailing tongue. But the more she tried to divert her line of thinking, the more her thoughts returned to him.

Leah now just wanted to fall asleep for the night and awake again—in the blink of an eye—to the cold light of day. Daytime seemed safer to her, somehow. Even if she had nightmares, and she was sure she would, at least they wouldn't be real.

Leah closed her eyes and concentrated on the steady rhythm of Alex's breathing, hoping that having something to focus on would help settle her nerves and let the exhaustion she felt claim her.

But, instead, her body locked in fear as she heard something.

A quiet laugh.

Or, more accurately, a cackle.

Leah's eyes flicked open, and she instinctively looked ahead to a dark corner of the room, to the area that the sudden sound had originated from. The only light afforded was minimal, borrowed by the moonlight outside that seeped in through the cracks of the curtains—not enough to pierce the shadows that seemed to engulf the corner.

She felt her breathing quicken as her heart pounded in her chest. All was silent again, but she was absolutely certain she had heard that menacing laugh.

Someone was in the room with her.

Alex still slept soundly on the inflatable matters at the foot of her bed. His breathing was steady and consistent. He was blissfully unaware of what Leah was experiencing.

Again, she heard it.

That low, old, feminine cackle emitting from the black.

Leah instinctively pulled the sheets up over her head and tucked her knees up to her chest. She hugged herself.

Go away. Go away. Go away.

With her heart in her mouth, she waited for the mocking laughter to return. At first, she could detect nothing.

Then, the creaking of a floorboard.

Leah tensed as she heard another creak. A definite footstep, coming from the same layer of space as the cackle she'd heard.

Closer and closer.

Step after step.

Her brow was sweating, and her throat felt as if it was closing up. She tried to scream, but only succeeded in letting out a small, almost inaudible cry.

The footsteps continued, constant and steady, until Danni heard them stop at the edge of the bed, just to her side. She then felt a shadow fall over her, as if someone was looking down on her.

Tears rolled down her cheeks, and she felt her body shake uncontrollably. She wanted to scream, but couldn't find her voice.

The cackling returned, and through the light cotton sheets she saw something move in the darkness above.

Something was reaching out for her.

Go away, go away, go away.

Her body tensed again, and then the sheet was suddenly pulled free, away from her.

Leaving her exposed.

Leah felt the cold air hit her body and instinctively

clamped her hands over her eyes. She waited for what came next.

She heard slow, laboured breathing. It grew louder, and she knew whoever was above her was now leaning in close. She could smell a horrible stench—like rotting cabbage—as the cold breath gently fell onto her skin, but she could not bring herself to remove her hands from her eyes.

She could not face the thing that was so close to her.

Leah began to sob, still wanting to scream, still wanting to make as much noise as she could to draw someone's attention, but her terrified body and vocal cords simply would not cooperate. She was frozen in fear.

Until the thing touched her.

An ice-cold hand clamped tightly around her wrist. In that instant, Leah's faculties jolted back into action. She quickly pulled her hand free and bolted upright, her eyes now fully open. The scream was still stuck in her throat, waiting to bellow free.

But Leah saw no one.

There was no one there, no one standing over her. And yet she could still feel the cold throb in her wrist from that firm grip.

It made no sense.

Was she going insane?

She began to sob, louder this time, and again curled herself up, aware that she was now exposed with no sheets to cover her. If she was going crazy, then how did that explain the sheets being clawed away from her?

She looked over the edge of the bed as saw Alex sleeping blissfully. She so badly wanted to wake him, to have some company, to help her get through this terror. Then she noticed the bedroom door, the one she was certain she had closed earlier. It was now ajar, a small gap revealing the hallway behind.

Leah froze. Her blood ran cold.

She saw someone though the small gap in the door; a hideous-looking old woman staring back at her from the corridor.

Leah saw hints of a long black dress buttoned up to a high-collared neck, and an almost-skeletal face with grey hair pulled up into a tight a bun. Leah also noticed that the old woman had unnaturally wide eyes, and a black, sinister, smile.

The cackle returned.

'No,' Leah said, still sobbing. She was about to scream, finally finding her voice, when movement drew her attention; Alex had sat up from his bed and was looking at her through sleepy eyes.

'Leah?' he asked in a soft voice.

Leah looked to him, then back to the opening, back to that horrible old woman.

But she was no longer there.

Leah could only see the dark corridor beyond.

'Leah, are you okay?' Alex pressed. 'What happened to your covers?'

Leah started to cry and again curled herself into a ball. Alex quickly moved over to her, bringing her discarded blanket with him. He slid onto the bed and cuddled next to her. She latched onto him as tightly as she could.

'What is it, Leah? What happened?'

She didn't answer him directly, because she didn't know what to say. She just wanted to go and wake her parents and get the hell out of there.

But she didn't. She simply hugged her brother. 'I'm scared,' she said.

'It's okay,' he replied, 'there's nothing to be scared of.'

That was their father's influence talking, not Alex. She sensed it in his tone. But right now, she didn't want that condescension. Leah just wanted to feel safe.

Alex pulled away from her and re-made the covers on the bed before tucking her in. For a moment, Leah felt a little ashamed. After all, it had always been her job to look after her younger sibling, not the other way around.

'Try to get some sleep,' he said, and Leah grabbed his arm.

'Don't sleep down there,' she said, though it was closer to a plea.

'Okay,' he replied and got into bed with her. Thankfully, he asked no further questions, seemingly aware that all she needed was his presence. Knowing someone was close made her feel a little better.

Though not much.

She didn't say anything else that night, but she did not sleep, either. Leah simply lay awake until dawn, constantly on edge.

Constantly expecting something else to show itself.

JON DREAMT that night of things he would not remember the next day. Of a place that should have been impossible. A hellish plane of demented, twisted existence.

Of pain and torture.

And the things that existed there were not human.

Was it hell?

Or something else?

Something more?

Something worse.

Though he would forget this dream come the morning, it would leave its mark.

And as he slept and dreamt, something hideous and inhuman stood by him in the night, whispering things to him...

10

Danni felt sick.

Not in a melodramatic way, or an exaggerated, butterflies in the tummy kind of way. She was actually struggling to keep from vomiting... again. The car ride to the small church had been touch-and-go, and she hoped that once they stopped moving and she got some air things would calm down.

No such luck.

After arriving, she stood in the church's car park leaning against the SUV, looking at the floor and the mess she'd left on it after throwing up.

Jon stroked her back.

'Are you okay, Mom?' Alex asked, and it struck Danni that they had been asking each other that question a lot this weekend. She didn't verbally answer, as she was afraid that opening her mouth would grant her body permission to purge her stomach again, so she just nodded. She wasn't okay, though. The reason she felt so sick was because her stomach was twisted into a tight, prickly knot. She was wracked with worry and apprehension at what she was about to go through.

Get it together, Danni.

Theirs was the only vehicle in the small car park. The church—St. Peters—was one of a few in town, but she remembered it well from her childhood. The small, stone church—with its accompanying graveyard—was situated close to her newly inherited property, a little farther along the same road, sitting just on the edges of the town's borders.

Near to the church was a small cluster of quaint houses and cottages, which were quite nice for the town, and the only other building of note was a single public house.

Danni's mother and father had been married at St. Peters, and she had been christened here, too, but the last time she had set foot on these grounds was during one of the saddest days of her life.

One that seemed to set in motion the years of misery that would follow.

Her mother was buried in the graveyard to the rear of the church, though Danni had rarely visited it back when she lived here. The idea crossed her mind that she should do so now.

One thing at a time.

She could do that when they finished dumping the body of her father into the ground.

Danni straightened up, feeling her stomach finally start to calm, though it was far from settled.

'Any better?' Jon asked.

'Yeah,' Danni said. 'A little. Just nerves, I guess.'

'It's understandable.'

A slight cough from behind alerted Danni to another presence approaching. She looked over her shoulder and saw an old, painfully thin man approaching. He had fine hair and a messy beard, both of which were pure white, and a kind face. He wore robes of the church.

She recognised him, but he was much older than she remembered.

'Father Atkins,' Danni said in way of greeting.

'Danielle Watson,' he said with a smile as he walked slowly over to them, clutching a Bible with hands that were crossed over his midsection.

He was the vicar who had married her parents, and who had christened her, and also the one who had laid her mother to rest. He seemed like a permanent fixture of the church—hell, of the town itself—however, age was now clearly catching up with him.

He held out a hand, which Danni took. She hoped he wouldn't see the patch of vomit she had left on the floor next to the car. If he had, he made no show of noticing.

'It's been a long time since I've seen you, Danielle,' he said. 'You were just a young girl back then. Now look at you; all grown up and,' he cast a glance at everyone, smiling, 'with a beautiful family. How are you?'

'I'm okay,' Danni said with a shrug. 'And it's Danni Morgan now. I'm not really looking forward to today, to be honest.'

'Understandable,' Father Atkins said, giving a solemn nod. 'Days such as today are never easy. But we get through them. And, I have a feeling you will be able to draw strength from the loved ones you have with you.' The old man then held his hand out to Jon, who shook it.

'I'm Jon, Jon Morgan,' Jon said.

'Nice to meet you. My name is Father Atkins. But please, call me Peter.'

'The pleasure is all mine, Peter.'

'And who are these?' he asked, making a theatrical show of opening his arms towards the children.

Leah, Danni had already noticed, looked exhausted.

'This is my eldest, Leah,' Danni said, 'and her younger brother, Alex.'

'Pleased to meet you both,' he said, shaking their hands. 'You certainly have the look of your mother, dear girl. I'm willing to bet you will grow up to be just as beautiful as her, if not more so.' Leah smiled shyly. 'And, may I ask,' Father Atkins went on, turning now to Alex, 'I see you have some walking aids there. Have you had an accident, young man?'

'No,' Alex said, shaking his head, 'I need them to walk sometimes. I was born with cerebral palsy. It affects my legs, so they aren't as strong as they should be.' When Alex spoke about his condition, it was never in a sad, self-pitying way. More matter of fact.

'Well,' Father Atkins said, 'I may not know you very well, young man, but it is clear from meeting you now that, even if your legs aren't as strong as you would like, your spirit seems unbreakable. That is marvellous and, I must say, much more important than being able to kick a football.'

'Thank you,' Alex said, smiling.

'Not at all.'

Danni found herself smiling as well. Father Atkins had always been a kind man who could put people at ease. Danni was also aware that her feeling of nausea had passed; the old man and his demeanour making her somewhat more comfortable.

'Shall we go inside?' he said, gesturing towards the small church.

'Shouldn't we wait for everyone else to arrive?' Jon said, looking around. The road beyond the church was quiet, deserted.

The old man looked briefly to the floor, then to Danni. 'I do not think anyone else will be coming. You see, your father very much kept to himself in his later years. So, I think today will be a more private, intimate affair.'

As nice as the man was, Danni knew sugar coating when she heard it, but found she did not care enough to probe any further.

'Okay,' she said, 'let's go.'

They followed Father Atkins inside. Danni's family flanked her on both sides: Jon to her right, holding her hand, and her children to her left. And, as much as she was dreading this, she did find strength in their presence—Father Atkins had been right about that.

They entered and took a seat in the row of pews at the front.

The church was small, could hold no more than maybe a hundred people. However, with only six present—including Father Atkins, and an old woman sitting at the organ—it felt empty and hollow.

The ceiling was quite high, with timber rafters criss-crossing each other. The walls were lined with tall, thin, stained-glass windows, which let through streams of distorted light. Rows of pews filled the central section and, to the front of these pews, there was a pulpit and lectern, where Father Atkins now stood.

There was a small chancel area just behind him, and this was where the plain wooden casket lay, its lid closed as per Danni's request.

Old Arthur had been here waiting for them.

No one had carried him in. He had not passed a gathering of mourners as would normally happen a funeral. And Danni knew the reason for that; no one wanted to take the evil old bastard on their shoulders.

What a sad and lonely way to exit this world.

No more than he deserved.

Jon put his hand on her leg to let her know he was there, but in all honesty, Danni barely noticed the gesture. She was focused solely on that coffin.

'Let us begin,' Father Atkins said, getting the service underway.

~

THE SERVICE WAS BRIEF, and Danni got the feeling that Father Atkins was only saying the bare minimum. There were a few hymns—that only he sang to—accompanied by the deep, booming tones of the organ, but he didn't have a lot to say about the deceased. That could have been because he hadn't been given any intimate details, but Danni seemed to sense some other cause for the brevity.

Maybe a personal reason?

The religious man looked at the coffin only a few times during his sermon, but when he did, Danni noticed the mask fall. In those moments, his expression was not that of a friendly man of God.

It was a brief look of disdain.

Danni hadn't known how she would react during the funeral, if she would cry or be upset, but her eyes were as dry as those of her family, who were here saying goodbye to a man they had never met. Still, the experience wasn't an easy one, and Danni found herself flip-flopping between feelings of pure anger, hurt, and self-pity.

Once finished, Father Atkins stated that they would now move to the graveyard outside, to take Mr. Watson to his final resting place. As they got to their feet, Danni saw four burly men in blue overalls emerge from a side door. These men, evidently, were the makeshift pallbearers.

Not that she could complain about their informality. She herself had attended her own father's funeral in nothing more than boots, jeans, a white tank top, blue over-shirt and coat. Hardly formal wear.

Her father didn't deserve the effort.

Father Atkins led them round to the back of the church, to what was a surprisingly large graveyard. Danni read a few of the tombstones as they walked and could see that the ones closest to the church, the ones that weren't weathered to the point of being illegible, were hundreds of years old.

Farther up ahead, she saw an open, freshly dug grave, ready and waiting to swallow up her father for the rest of time. She took Jon's hand in her own as they stood at the edge, waiting for the pallbearers to catch up with them.

It was here, standing at the edge of the grave, that Danni felt the worst of the anger course through her. Not just anger at what her father had done, but anger at where he would be buried. Danni cast her eyes to the left of the open grave, to the grave of her mother; its marble headstone now starting to weather. The surrounding grass was a little over-grown, and there were no flowers or items of remembrance around the plot.

It looked abandoned.

She felt a pang of sadness and guilt, but it was overshadowed by white-hot fury as the men arrived with her father.

He didn't deserve to be laid here.

Not next to her.

Danni watched as the men carefully lowered the coffin, and it sunk farther and farther into the ground.

Sink all the way to hell, you bastard.

She felt Jon's arm slip round her waist and hold her tight, which snapped her from her thoughts. It was only then, she realised, that tears were running freely down her face. The floodgates had opened, and she began sobbing uncontrollably.

Why am I crying for him?

It didn't make any sense. She should be glad he was gone. The cause of all her childhood misery was now literally disappearing into the ground, out of her life.

For good.

And yet, amongst the anger and hate, she did notice a slight twinge of sadness and regret.

She found herself focusing on the earlier days.

Arthur's warm smile.

Reading to her at night. Kissing her on the forehead before switching off the light.

I love you, sweet-pea. Sleep tight.

Before Mother died.

Before he changed.

Father Atkins read another passage from the Bible, and the makeshift pallbearers threw dirt onto the casket.

Dust to dust.

Danni, against her will, let out a small, audible cry. Jon hugged her even tighter, and she felt her children gather around her as well. All were there for her, all lending her their strength.

Was it her fault that her father had turned out like he had? Had she somehow done this to him? Maybe he needed her after Mom had died and she hadn't been there for him. Maybe he needed someone to lend him their strength in his time of need, like her family was doing for her now.

Is that what had turned him into such a monster?

After the service ended, they returned to the front car

park accompanied by Father Atkins. Danni had somewhat regained her composure, and they stood close to the SUV.

'Thank you for the service,' Danni said.

'Do not mention it, Danielle,' Father Atkins replied with a humble bow. 'You have been very brave. I know today couldn't have been easy.'

'Harder than expected,' Danni said, turning to look out over the field opposite them. It was then she saw another car on the otherwise empty road, parked to the side. A young woman who seemed to be in her late twenties stood by the car. Her messy hair was blowing in the wind, and she was staring daggers at them.

It wasn't a face Danni was familiar with.

'Who is that?' Danni asked. Father Atkins looked up, and his face dropped.

'Oh, no one,' he said.

'It isn't *no one*,' Danni pressed. 'Did she want to attend today? Should we have waited?'

'No,' he said. 'No, I don't think she would have wanted to attend.'

'Father,' Danni said, firmly, 'what is it? What aren't you telling me?'

She could see the conflict evident on his face as he chewed at the inside of his left cheek. Eventually, he placed a hand to her left elbow and gently guided her a few steps away from her family, clearly wanting to speak in private. Danni knew her family would be interested in hearing what was going on, but thankfully they gave her some privacy.

'It was something I was hoping I wouldn't need to tell you,' the man said, quietly.

'What is?'

'Things about your father. Things that would be better dying with him.'

'Tell me,' Danni said, finding herself eager to know more.

'It isn't pleasant,' he said, still chewing on his cheek.

'Father, there was a reason I left this place. I'm under no illusions about what kind of man my father was.'

'It wasn't always this way,' Father Atkins said quickly, 'but your father is not someone many in this area will miss.'

'What did he do? Did something happen to that girl?'

Father Atkins nodded. 'Yes. Her name is Annie. Annie Burton. A few years ago she was delivering leaflets—something to do with her mother's business, I think—and she came up here to drop one off at your father's house. Needless, really; your father was little more than a recluse at that point. But when she pushed the leaflet through the door, he opened it and asked her inside. Said he needed help with something. Unfortunately, she went inside—'

'Why?' Danni asked. 'She didn't know him, why would she go into the house of a stranger like that?'

'To help an old man, Danielle,' Father Atkins replied. 'She said afterward that he had looked distressed. So she went inside to help.'

'What happened?'

'I do not know everything,' the man said, 'only snippets of the story from different people, and what little Annie told me herself. But once inside, she says he attacked her.'

'He what?'

'He threw himself at her, and by all accounts was quite violent. She was lucky to escape. But the experience wasn't without its trauma for her. That, I suspect, is why she is here today. Possibly some kind of closure.'

That was something Danni could relate to.

'I never knew,' she said.

'There was no way you could. Danni, I'm not sure what

happened in his life to make your father change into what he became, but what's done is done. You have a family of your own now, and your focus should be on your children. Be everything to them you didn't have yourself. Try not to dwell too much on the ghosts of the past.'

'Easier said than done, Father,' Danni said.

He placed a hand on her shoulder. 'But it *can* be done. Now, I have things to attend to, but if you need me for anything you know where I am. Be well, Danielle. It was good to see you again.'

'Thank you,' Danni said, resting her hand on his. He smiled and nodded before walking back to the church. Danni looked over to her family who stood waiting patiently for her. She then looked over to the mysterious woman by the road.

Danni decided that she wanted to know more.

11

'Is everything okay?' Jon asked Danni as she walked back over to her family.

Danni nodded. 'Yeah, it's fine. I just want to go talk with that girl over there. Apparently she knew my dad.'

'She did?' Jon asked, sounding a little surprised. 'Why didn't she come to the service?'

'That's what I want to find out,' Danni lied.

'I'll come with you.'

'No,' Danni insisted. 'I'll be fine. And I won't be long. You just wait here for me.'

She gave her husband no opportunity to argue the point. She spun on her heels and walked over to the girl, who looked more than a little apprehensive as Danni approached.

The car that Annie Burton stood close to was an old model VW Golf, one that seemed to have seen plenty of miles. The girl herself was wearing simple clothes: black trousers, and a purple woollen jumper beneath a black over-coat. Though she was pretty, she didn't seem to take much care in her appearance, with uncombed hair, no makeup, and dark rings under her eyes.

'Annie Burton?' Danni asked, stopping at the church's boundary. A low, shin-height, random-stone wall separated them. When addressed, Annie seemed to twitch.

'How do you know my name?' she asked.

'Father Atkins told me,' Danni said. 'I'm Danni.' She held out her hand over the wall, but the woman just looked at it like it was some kind of foreign object. Danni smiled and withdrew her arm.

'Why are you here?' the woman asked.

'At the funeral?'

'Yes. I didn't think anyone would miss *him*.'

'Well, you might be right about that. But I'm his daughter, so I had to come.'

The woman's eyes opened a little wider. 'Daughter? I didn't know he had any family.'

'Well, I left when I was young, and I haven't been back since. Can I ask why you're here?' Annie looked away and didn't answer immediately.

'I wanted to make sure,' she eventually said. 'To make sure he was gone.'

'He is gone,' Danni said. 'I can promise you that.'

'Good,' Annie said, venom lacing her voice. 'Lasting this long was more than he deserved.'

'Annie,' Danni went on, trying to be as soft and tactful as possible, 'Father Atkins mentioned that something happened between you and my dad. That he attacked you, somehow?'

Annie turned her scowling eyes to Danni. Her top lip curled. 'It wasn't Father Atkins' business to say that.'

'Okay,' Danni said, holding out her palms defensively. 'I

don't mean to cause offence, I just want to know what happened.'

'Why do you care?'

Danni hesitated, then went on. 'Because I know what it's like, having my father's shadow hanging over you. There's a reason I ran away from here. I know what kind of person he really was, Annie.'

'What do you mean?'

'Exactly what I said. When I was younger, he... did things to me. I'm not here out of mourning, but because I have to be. To get closure. So, really, I think we're both here for the same reason.'

Upon hearing that, Annie's tensed body visibly relaxed, and the worried frown on her face eased a little. 'I'm sorry to hear that,' she said. 'Must be hard, knowing that your father was such a monster.'

The comment, for reasons she couldn't explain, actually bothered Danni. She felt defensive, as if it was insinuated she could be that type of person as well. Guilt by association. She didn't let it show.

'Annie, please tell me what happened.'

Annie looked down to the floor, shifting from one foot to the other. 'A few years ago, I went up to his house. I was delivering some fliers for my mother. She'd started a hairdressing business and asked me to help get some leaflets out. I wasn't planning on going to that house, to be honest, it always gave me the creeps. I just wanted to come and hit the other houses up here, but I passed it on the way and I figured it would be another leaflet done. I was in a hurry to get finished, and I thought, why not? So, I went up the drive and pushed one through the door.'

'Then what happened?'

'Almost as soon as the letter box closed, the door swung

open. Your father was standing there, looking angry. He asked me who I was and what I was doing there. So I told him. Then his face changed. I can't explain it, but the anger vanished, and he just turned around and started to walk back inside, with the door still open. He shouted for me to follow him.'

'And you went?'

'Not at first. He disappeared into one of the rooms and called out for me again. Said he needed help with something. It was weird, and I was going to turn around and walk away, but he shouted again. Said he was having chest pains, and his phone wasn't working. I wanted to leave, but after hearing that, I couldn't. I didn't know if he was telling the truth, but I knew if he was, and I left, I'd never be able to live with myself. And if he was lying, well, I figured he was so old that I could get away if I needed to.'

Annie trailed off, so Danni prompted her to continue. 'Go on.'

'So I went in. I kept the front door open and walked into the same room he'd disappeared into, which was the living room. He was sitting in an old chair, looking out the window with a smile on his face. Not a nice smile, either. I asked him what sort of pain he was having in his chest but he just ignored me. Stayed quiet. I asked him again, but it was like he was blanking me. I knew then that something was up, so I said I was going to leave.'

Again, Annie stopped talking, and this time she started tearing up. The memory was clearly a painful one. Something else Danni could relate to. 'What happened, Annie?' Danni asked, trying to sound patient and understanding.

'I turned to leave,' Annie said, her voice cracking, 'but he was up and out of that chair faster than he should have been able to. He grabbed me from behind by the throat. His other arm wrapped around me. He was so strong. You couldn't tell by looking at him, but I've never felt anything like it. I couldn't budge. Then he started cursing at me. Real vile things, too. His face was so close, I could smell the alcohol on him. He kept calling me a cunt, telling me what he was going to do to me...'

Annie shook her head and held up her hand, indicating she was done. But Danni didn't want her to be done, she wanted—no, needed—to know the rest of the story.

'Jesus,' she said to the girl, 'that's horrible. How did you get away?'

Annie took a moment. Tears were now freely streaming down her face.

'I fought. I kicked at him and squirmed and tried everything I could to get away. In the end, I grabbed grabbed his testicles. It was disgusting to do, but I was desperate—I squeezed as hard as I could and just about crushed them. Eventually, he let me go. And I ran.'

'I'm so sorry you had to go through that,' Danni said, though she sensed there was more to the story. Annie was biting her bottom lip and rocking back and forth slightly on her heels. 'Is there anything else?'

Annie shook her head. 'No, I ran out of the house after that.'

Danni didn't believe it. 'You can tell me,' she said. 'I won't judge you. It's okay, I swear, you can tell me.'

Annie squinted at her, tears still filling her eyes. There was something there, something that had been eating away at the girl.

'I saw... something,' she said. Her voice was uneven, quiet as a whisper. 'In the house.'

That statement gripped Danni. 'What? What do you mean? What did you see?'

'You won't believe me,' Annie replied. 'I haven't told anyone because it's crazy.'

'Try me. After this weekend, I don't think anything can sound crazy.'

Annie gave her a confused look. 'Are you staying at the house?'

Danni nodded. 'I am, with my family. So please, tell me what you saw. I'll believe it, I swear.'

Her thoughts were of Alex and Leah, and what had happened to them the previous day.

'I ran into the hallway,' Annie said, 'and was just about to leave when, I swear to God, the door closed in my face. Completely on its own. I was running so fast I ran straight into it. And no matter how hard I tried, I couldn't get it back open. That's when your father walked in from the living room. His face had... changed, somehow. His eyes were different. I know it doesn't make sense, but it was like there was something in him that just wanted to hurt me and make me suffer. And he had this awful smile on his lips. Then I looked up the stairs...'

Again, she trailed off, and Danni felt a momentary flash of anger. She just wanted the girl to keep going. She knew that was harsh, and that this woman was reliving something terrible, but Danni desperately needed to know.

'What? What did you see?'

'A woman. An old woman. She was standing right at the top of the stairs and was wearing a black dress. She had the same kind of eyes as your dad. Dark. Sinister. And I knew—I just *knew*—that she wasn't a real person. Not the same way you and I are. She was something else.'

'You mean, you thought she was a ghost?'

The woman nodded and wiped her eyes. 'I told you it was crazy. You don't believe me, do you?'

'I do,' Danni said, not sure if that was true or not. It was a fantastical story, one that she would have normally taken as the ramblings of a troubled person. Or a liar. But after last night, she wasn't quite so sure. 'Then what happened?'

'I kept banging at the door, but it wouldn't budge. Your father was still coming forward, towards me, and that... woman just started to laugh. I panicked and tried to get past him, to escape out the back, but he grabbed my coat. I slipped out of it and ran into the kitchen. I didn't even try the back door, I just grabbed a chair and broke a window with it, then climbed out. Cut myself all to hell.' She pulled her coat sleeve back to show her arm. Danni saw that the skin was streaked with scars.

'And you managed to get away?' Danni asked.

'Just barely. Your dad nearly caught me again, but I got out in time. But there was something else as well. After I ran around the side of the house, I looked over to that big stone building—'

'The mill?' Danni asked.

'Yeah. The door to it was open. And there was something looking out from inside.'

She stopped again, crying, this time burying her head into her hands.

'Another one of those things?' Danni asked.

'No,' Annie said, her voice muffled by her hands. She pulled her head up, revealing a face that had grown red. 'This was something different. I don't know what it was, but I knew I needed to get away from it. Being around your dad and that old woman was bad enough, but this... this was different. Just looking at it made me more terrified than I was when I was inside the house with your dad.'

'What did it look like?'

'It doesn't matter,' Annie said, stepping away. 'The

important thing is that your dad is dead. So, hopefully, the nightmares will stop, and whatever *it* was died there with him.'

'Please,' Danni said, 'I need to know more. Don't go.'

The woman opened the car door, still sobbing. 'There's no more to say. I've told you everything.'

'But there has to be more,' Danni said, pleading. 'What was the thing in the mill? Did it do anything, say anything?'

'No,' Annie said and got into the car, shutting the door behind her. The window was already open and she looked out to Danni as she started the engine. 'You need to get your family out of that place. It isn't safe. There is something evil there. And it'll kill you all.'

She then put the engine into gear and drove away, leaving Danni stunned.

12

THE JOURNEY back to the house was a quiet one.

Jon had asked Danni what the conversation she'd had with the woman was about, but she didn't answer, instead drawing into herself. He wanted to press the matter with her, as it had clearly upset her, but, given that she had just come away from her father's funeral—and was obviously upset—he decided to leave it be.

For now.

He knew that heading back to the house wouldn't really help his wife's mood either, so when they approached the turnoff for the house, he simply kept on going.

'You missed the turn, Dad,' Alex said from the back seat.

'I know,' Jon replied, 'but I thought we could do with spending a little time together away from all this.'

'What did you have in mind?' Danni asked, turning to face him.

'It might not be the best place in the world, but I'm sure we can find somewhere in this town that has nice food. And not pizza this time. A proper meal. Sound good?'

'It does to me,' Alex said.

'Yeah,' Danni agreed. 'Yeah, it does.'

They drove to town, to the relatively large car park in the centre of the square. It gave them a panoramic view of the whole area, allowing them to see what it had to offer.

They found a spot and got out of the SUV and Jon noticed that Leah, seemingly lost in her own world, did not make her usual bee-line to help Alex. The incident in the shower last night was obviously still playing on her mind. If Jon was being completely honest with himself, that disappointed him a little.

Though could he really blame her? She was still young —he needed to remember that. Hell, he'd had his own incident as well. One that, for a split second, had him considering the unthinkable: that something had pushed him. Of course, that was rubbish, and he'd admonished himself for even entertaining the idea. Still, a little time away from that house would be good for them all.

He walked to the rear door and helped Alex disembark before retrieving the boy's crutches for him. Out of the corner of his eye, he saw Leah take notice, and her face flushed; clearly a little embarrassed about not helping her brother.

'Anywhere look good?' Jon asked.

While there weren't any restaurants around, per se, he did spot some pubs and figured a few of them would offer Sunday lunch.

'How about that one?' Alex asked, pointing a crutch to a public house in the centre of the square, aptly called The Old Mill. Out of the meagre selection available, it looked the most appealing, with a new render to its outer walls, clean windows, and a sleek sign with cursive font. It had clearly benefited from a recent makeover, which hopefully meant the food would be good.

'Looks fine to me,' Jon said. He looked to Danni and Leah for approval. 'Everyone agree?'

Danni and Leah glanced at each other first, as if sharing a telepathic link. Without a word spoken between them, a consensus seemed to have been formed.

'Let's go,' Danni said.

DANNI REMEMBERED THE OLD MILL, but back in her day it had been known as The Fox Cub, and it had changed drastically since she had last been inside. It was the first place she'd ever bought an alcoholic drink, and it had been known in the village as being quite lenient in regards to who they served. This drew a younger crowd, many underage, getting them acquainted with the main pastime for adults in towns like this: drinking.

It was a completely different place now. The grimy carpets and stained, faded seats had all been replaced and upgraded. More than half the bar was set up with tables and chairs, and the place was more food oriented with only a small section designated as bar. The decor inside was now light and airy: lots of whites and magnolias, as opposed to the grungy feel she remembered from her youth, drinking the night away instead of going home to her father. Danni thought the place now bordered on being trendy.

A polite young girl who didn't look much older than Leah approached and asked if they were intending to order food. Jon said they did, and she asked them to take a seat.

'Anywhere specific?' Jon asked.

'Oh,' she said with a big smile, 'just sit wherever you

want. The menus are on the table, so just decide what you want then come up to the bar and order when you're ready.'

'No problem,' Jon said, but Danni knew he would have preferred being seated and having a waiter come over to take their order.

But Danni was just relieved that they didn't have to go straight back to that house. Annie's story was still fresh in her mind, and she was conflicted about what to do. She remembered the rather ominous warning.

You need to get your family out of that place.
It isn't safe. There is something evil there.
And it'll kill you all.

Maybe the girl was crazy—that would be the most logical explanation, the one Jon would cling to—but when it came to her family's safety, Danni wasn't so sure she could just ignore it so easily. The simple fact was, she didn't want her family going back there. They would have to get their stuff, sure, but after that she wanted to be gone. However, she knew she would be at odds with Jon on that. It was already getting late in the day, so driving all the way home tonight was out of the question. That left the option of staying at a hotel or a bed and breakfast for the night, but she wasn't sure how amenable he would be to that idea, either, given the whole *stop running from the past* pilgrimage he had insisted she go through.

They took a seat in the corner of the pub, one that had a view of the town square from a large sash window, and started to peruse the menu. While doing so, Danni took a moment to look around and see if she could spot anyone she recognised. Not that she particularly wanted to reconnect with anyone—it was more of a general curiosity.

There were a few families eating their meals, and one looked a little familiar, but not enough to strike up conversation. It was a family of five: what she assumed was a husband and wife, with two children—both younger than Alex—and an elderly woman who was seated in a wheelchair. It was the old lady that Danni remembered, and then it fell into place; she used to be a teacher at Danni's old primary school. Although, Danni couldn't quite recall her name.

There were other people dotted around in the bar area as well, and again some faces were vaguely familiar, like fuzzy echoes from her past.

'Anything look appetising?' Jon asked the kids.

Alex smiled. 'They do pizza, that looks good.'

Jon laughed. 'You had pizza last night, pick something else.'

'I'll have the spaghetti, then.'

'A good choice. Leah?'

'Same,' Leah said and set the menu down. Danni noted that her daughter had barely even looked at the menu before deciding. The poor girl seemed weary and exhausted, so Danni made a mental note to get her alone and talk with her, to see if she could help. It wasn't fair to put her through this. Whatever was really going on back at the house, the fact that it was affecting Leah like this meant, at least to Danni, they needed to fix it and get far away from the source of agitation.

And that meant she needed to have a conversation with Jon away from the children and put her foot down.

'Okay,' Jon said, 'How about you, Danni? Don't tell me you're having spaghetti as well.' He was trying to keep the tone light and jovial, to counter the somber atmosphere that was hanging over them. That wasn't the way to fix this, though.

'I'll have a burger,' she said.

'And I'll go with the hunter's chicken. And for drinks?'

Everyone ordered a lemonade, with only Alex showing any kind of enthusiasm. 'No problem,' Jon said. 'I'll go and order.'

He got up and walked over to the bar, taking a menu with him. Danni saw her chance. 'Wait here,' she said to her children, 'I just want to talk to your dad about something.'

She got to her feet and approached the bar as well, arriving just as Jon was finishing up with the order.

'I'll go get your drinks, and your food will be out shortly,' said the same barmaid that had greeted them earlier.

Jon turned and looked a little surprised to see Danni next to him. 'Change your mind about the burger?' he asked.

She shook her head. 'No, it isn't that,' she said, her tone serious.

His face took on a look of concern. 'What is it? Everything okay?'

'It's just,' Danni started, taking a moment to choose her words, 'the house. And us staying in it.'

'What do you mean?'

'I mean, it's putting a lot of stress on us. I get why we are staying there, I do, and it was a good idea at the time. But now, I dunno, I just think we should consider staying someplace else tonight before we head home tomorrow.'

Jon rolled his eyes and let out a sigh. 'Are you serious?'

'Yes, Jon, I am. Have you seen your daughter over there? She looks like she hasn't slept a wink. She's scared, Jon, and she's exhausted. There's no reason to make her stay another night in a place we know she doesn't like.'

'Come on, Danni,' Jon said, 'there's nothing to be scared of. She got herself spooked and confused. That's all. It's not a good enough reason to run away.'

'What do you mean *run away*? I just don't want to put our daughter through more stress.'

'There's nothing stressful about it, other than what's in her head. And if we leave, then that *is* running away. Running from nothing. Jesus, Danni, what are we teaching our kids if we let them get scared of their own shadow?'

'Jon, that's not it, it's just—'

'No, Danni,' he snapped, cutting her off. 'It's just nothing. I'm not having it. There's a reason we are here. Leah is a big girl, not a child, she has to learn the difference between imagination and reality. Frankly, I really thought she was too old for this kind of thing.'

'How can you say that? Something really got to her, and you're just dismissing it like it's nothing.'

'Danni,' he said, putting a hand on her shoulder, 'it *is* nothing. That's exactly what it is. And she can't go through life like that.'

'And what about me?' Danni asked, trying a different tactic.

'What about you?'

'Did you ever stop to think how staying in that house would affect me? Do you know what I went through there when I was growing up?'

She started to raise her voice a little, just as the barmaid was returning with the drinks. The girl set them in front of Jon and gave an uncomfortable, closed-mouthed smile. She then moved quickly away, leaving them to it.

'Of course I do,' Jon said, sounding now a little less confrontational. 'But that's the whole reason we decided to do this.'

'*You* decided to do this,' Danni said, pushing Jon's hand from her shoulder. 'You decided it would be best for me and didn't listen when I said I was uncomfortable.'

'Danni, I know it's hard, but come on, have you ever really dealt with what happened to you?'

'How the hell do you deal with something like that?' She raised her voice even more, anger taking over. This wasn't a discussion to Danni anymore, it was an argument. She was aware the children were looking over, but couldn't help herself—she couldn't ease off or let it go. 'And you know something else? This isn't your problem to fix. I'll deal with it in my own way.'

'Not my problem to fix? You're my wife, Danni. Your problems are my problems.'

'Not this one,' she said, gritting her teeth. 'You don't just visit an old house where bad things happened and suddenly everything is okay. What happened left scars, Jon. Scars that will stay with me forever. That's just the way it is.'

'But it doesn't have to be—'

'Stop it!' she said, shouting. 'Just stop trying to fix everything with your fucking logic. This isn't a logical thing. So just stop it and be supportive. That's all you need to do for me. Just back me up when I say I don't want to stay in that fucking house anymore!'

Jon looked shocked at her outburst. He didn't respond and was either stuck for something to say or was considering her words. She hoped it was the latter.

It seemed like it was.

'Please,' she said, lowering her voice and stepping closer to him. 'Just support me. And support your daughter. We need to get away from that place.'

He tensed up. 'What do you mean? Why do you say that?'

'I told you, I'm not comfortable there.'

He studied her face, making Danni want to look away. 'That isn't it,' he said. 'There's something else, something in your voice. What did that woman say at the cemetery, Danni?'

'Nothing important,' Danni said.

'Then why avoid it? Why not tell me?'

'It doesn't matter.'

'Then just tell me.'

He had a thread now, Danni realised, something to pull on. And she knew he wouldn't let it go. He'd picked up on the urgency of her wanting to get out of the house, something beyond just her unease. She cursed herself for pushing too hard, as he'd seemed ready to relent.

'Something happened to her,' Danni said. 'She said that my dad attacked her. That's it.'

Jon's eyes narrowed. 'In the house?'

Danni nodded. 'Yes.'

'Was it serious?'

'Of course it was. How is an attack not serious?'

'Did he hurt her?'

'A little, but she managed to get away.'

'Odd. After you spoke to her, you were really shaken up, Danni. I know finding out something like that about your dad would have been a bit of a shock, but considering what kind of person your father was, is it really that much of a surprise? What aren't you telling me?'

'Nothing,' Danni said, suddenly feeling her words were futile.

'Just tell me. You want me to be supportive? Then you have to be honest with me.'

Danni sighed, not wanting to divulge that information, but she saw no other option. 'She said she saw something in the house.'

'Something?'

'An old woman watching her.' Danni hung her head as she spoke. 'And something else too. Something in the mill.'

'An old woman? And some*thing* in the mill? Are you saying what I think you are, Danni?' It was now his turn to raise his voice.

Danni noticed a middle-aged man in a suit-jacket approach them from behind the bar. 'It doesn't matter,' she said again, wanting Jon to focus on what was important.

'I don't believe this,' he said, throwing his hands up in the air.

'Excuse me,' the man in the jacket interjected. His name badge read: Tom Reed, Duty Manager. 'I'm going to have to ask you to please keep your voices down.'

'Did you honestly believe what she was telling you, Danni? Please tell me you didn't.'

Danni couldn't think of anything else to say, other than to yet again repeat herself. 'That doesn't matter. It isn't what's important.'

'It does matter,' Jon said. 'And it's exactly what's important.'

'Excuse me,' the duty manager repeated, more forcefully this time. 'If you don't return to your table now and lower your voices, I am going to have to ask you to leave. Understand?'

Danni saw that Jon looked visibly disappointed in her. Neither of them spoke.

'Do you understand?' the duty manager asked again.

Jon nodded. 'We do,' he said, and scooped up all four glasses, pressing them together and linking his fingers around them. He walked back over to the table without saying another word to Danni.

The duty manager was looking at her now, eyebrows raised.

'I'm sorry,' she said, not meaning it, and returned to the table.

The children looked worried and surprised. Danni and Jon didn't fight often, and never in front of the kids.

The food came shortly after, and they ate in complete silence.

13

Jon didn't like it.

The whole idea of turning tail and fleeing over what amounted to no more than a ghost story was preposterous. More than that, it would completely negate any progress Danni had made this weekend fighting off the only demons in this world that were real: personal ones.

And those could be overcome, provided you faced up to them.

He didn't like that Danni was upset, and he had known this weekend was going to be intensely difficult for her, but the fact was he knew she could get through it. She was strong enough, and it infuriated him that she couldn't see it for herself.

The drive back to the house had been as quiet as the dinner they'd eaten at the pub, and Jon could feel the sense of unease and uncertainty hanging over the entire family. The children had obviously heard the argument and would be in limbo about what was going to happen—were they going to stay or go?

It was only one more night, and he had no intention of leaving. At least until morning.

As it turned out, however, Danni wasn't quite finished.

No sooner had they returned to the house and entered the hallway when Danni spoke. 'Kids, go into the living room, please. Dad and I need to talk.'

Jon felt himself bristle. He didn't want to talk, he wanted to be done with the whole conversation. Leah and Alex filtered quietly into the living room, and Danni walked to the kitchen. 'A word, please,' she said to him, her voice even but stern.

Here we go again.

Jon followed her, and they each took a position in the kitchen; Danni leaning against one of the kitchen units, and Jon a few feet in front of her.

Both had their arms folded over their chests.

'Okay,' he said, resolving to keep his calm, 'where do we start?'

Danni took a breath, clearly trying to keep her emotions in check as well. 'Look, I understand where you're coming from, I really do, but everyone is miserable here. I'm not saying I believe that girl, at all, but that doesn't change the fact that staying here is the wrong thing to do.'

'Difficult doesn't mean wrong, Danni.'

'No, not always, but sometimes we need to stop and think if the difficulty is worth it. I mean, really, what are we hoping to get from staying here? I've come back, dealt with what had to be dealt with, and we watched them finally throw my dad into the ground. It's done. Mission accomplished.'

'So, where would we go? We can't drive all the way home tonight, it's too late and would take too long.'

'A hotel.'

'And what if Leah sees a shadow there that freaks her out? Do we run away again in the middle of the night and find somewhere else? And what if she thinks she sees someone back home, in our house? Do we move, just so she doesn't have to face up to being an adult? Is that what you are saying?'

Danni clenched her teeth together. 'Why are you being like this?' she asked. 'You know that's not what I'm saying.'

'But it is,' he said. 'Right now it's this house, but it could easily be somewhere else next. All that you're teaching them by capitulating is that the best way to solve a problem is to run away from it.'

'Come on, Jon, that's not what I'm saying at all. This is different.'

'It isn't different, Danni. It's a perfect example of what we need to weed out of them.'

'Weed out?'

'Yes. I won't have my children growing up to be cowards, to be scared of make-believe. If things get tough, they need to learn how deal with it head on. I won't have them turn into the type of people who run away from everything.'

That comment stung, and he saw Danni's face twist into an angry frown. 'What is that supposed to mean? Was that aimed at me?'

'No,' he said, shaking his head. 'That wasn't what I meant.'

'Bullshit. It's exactly what you meant. Do you think I run away from everything?'

'Danni, come on.'

'Answer the question, Jon. Do you think that?'

He took his time in answering. 'You don't run away from everything, but sometimes you don't exactly face things head on.'

'I can't believe you,' she said through gritted teeth. 'You think I should have just hung around here? Lived with my dad, knowing the kind of man he was?'

'No,' Jon said, steeping forward and gently taking hold of her arms. He felt her recoil slightly, but he held her firm. 'I told you, I don't blame you for that. But you have to admit, it's led you to repeat that pattern in life.'

'Meaning?'

'Come on, Danni. Remember our first-ever argument? It was nothing, but enough for you to say we were done. You ran for the hills, remember? And that would have been it had I not fought for us and changed your mind. Running was your first instinct, to protect yourself. How about when Alex was being picked on at school? You wanted to string the bullies up, which I admired, but also wanted to move him to a different school as well. It isn't healthy.'

'So I'm a coward?'

'No, but given what's happened in your life, I think you have a tendency to look for the easiest solution. The quick way out. It's understandable, Danni, of course it is, but we can change that.'

Danni laughed, but it sounded bitter, and she stepped away from him. 'There you go again,' she said. 'You know what? If we're dishing out home truths, maybe you should know a few.'

He sighed and shook his head. *This ought to be good.* 'Okay then, go ahead. Get it off your chest.'

'For one, you aren't a fucking doctor or a therapist. You think you are, and you think you know how to fix everything, but the reality is that you don't know shit.'

He shook his head again and looked away, not taking the comment seriously. 'Okay,' he said. 'Anything else?'

'You're damn right there is,' she said. 'I think this whole

thing has less to do with trying to help me, and more about you and your ego.'

That comment shocked him. How the hell could she think that? 'Is that right? And why is that, Danni? Why on earth would I want to stay here any longer than I have to?'

'Because you want to be seen as the one that solves everything. You like to know you're right. You thought this would be good for me, so no matter what I think, this is what we do, because you think it'll work. You can't possibly imagine that you could be wrong about anything. It doesn't even enter your fucking head. You're so damn arrogant. And, sometimes, utterly clueless as well.'

'I'm clueless, am I?' Jon said and stepped forward. Those words stung.

Because they weren't fucking true. Who does she think she is?

'Yes, you are. If you were any kind of man, you'd put aside your own ego and just do what's best for your family. But you can't, can you? It's pathetic.'

He walked closer, now nose to nose with her, nostrils flaring. She didn't back down, and that, for some reason, angered him even more.

'Pathetic? Really?' His voice bubbled with rage. 'The only thing pathetic about all of this is a grown woman believing in the boogeyman. A mother so cowardly that she's happy to push those fantasies on to her children and doesn't care what will happen so long as she doesn't have to face up to things. Scared little girl who has thrown her toys out of the pram because she isn't allowed to run away. Well boo-hoo, Danni. Grow the fuck up.'

Jon heard the crack before he felt it. Then his face started to sting, and he realised she had slapped him.

'Fuck you,' she said, seething with rage. She stormed back into the hallway.

'Running again?' he yelled and strode after her. 'Typical. Well, I can tell you this much, we aren't going anywhere tonight. So deal with it.'

She stomped up the stairs, but didn't reply. Jon saw that tears had pooled in her eyes. He started to go up after her, furious, but stopped halfway.

He knew pushing the matter further would only cause things to escalate, so he swallowed the rage that was building inside of him and watched her disappear down the hallway.

A door slammed.

With a sigh, Jon turned back to descend the stairs. As he did, he saw that both Leah and Alex were watching him from the living room door.

And both looked scared.

14

ALEX WAS TROUBLED.

He had known today was going to be hard, especially on his mother, but he never expected it to devolve into this. He could barely remember seeing his parents squabble, let alone have an all-out row. And it had gotten so bad that he'd heard his mother actually slap his father, the stinging impact ringing out even into the living room.

After his mother had run upstairs, his father had entered the room. Jon looked at Leah first, then to Alex.

'I take it you both heard all of that?'

Alex nodded.

'And back at the restaurant, as well,' Leah said. 'You two never fight.'

'I know,' Jon said. 'Today's just a little stressful for us all.'

'More so for Mom,' Leah said, nailing her colours to the mast. 'So why don't we support her and just go?'

Jon held up his hand, palm towards her. 'Stop,' he said, making it sound like a command. 'I'm not going to have this argument with you as well. Understand?'

Leah hesitated, then nodded.

'Good,' Jon said. 'Let's give your mother a little time. Just keep yourselves busy for a while until she comes back down. We only have another night, then we will be going home.'

Alex understood his father's position. It made no sense to get scared of things that weren't real. He knew that, and he wanted to make sure his father could see it. However, seeing how his mother and sister were in this place, he couldn't help but think that maybe, just maybe, it wasn't in their best interest to stay.

Leah walked over to a single chair close to the fireplace and dropped into it. She pulled out her earbuds, tapped on her phone, and listened to music. Evidently, this was going to be her way to pass the time until their mother came back down: by ignoring her father and simply not speaking.

Jon shrugged and looked to Alex. 'Want the tablet, Son?'

'Sure.'

Jon walked from the room. Alex heard him go into the kitchen and rustle around in one of their bags. He reappeared with the tablet and a book. He handed the electrical device to Alex and they both took a seat on the sofa.

Alex went to open one of the pre-loaded books on the device, but stopped when he saw something in the top corner of the screen—the 'No Service' message had changed to a single bar of signal.

He opened his internet browser to test the strength and, though it took a while, the home page eventually loaded.

His normal routine would have been to check the NASA website, then social media, but this time he had an urge to do something different. Though he knew none of it was real, he couldn't say he wasn't at least curious about Leah's experience last night. And, if he was being honest, his own as well. He could still remember the old woman he saw yesterday.

Thought he saw.

And Alex was intrigued to learn a little more about Bishops Hill.

He looked around, making sure both Leah and his father were occupied, and typed the phrase *Bishops Hill* into the search engine. The results page was agonisingly slow in loading, and the first link was the Wikipedia page.

He clicked on it.

More loading, then he was given a little information about the town: its population, when it was founded, and a section that caught his eye; *The Bishops Hill Murders.*

It was only a brief segment, but outlined a series of deaths in the town.

Horrible atrocitities, in a place that looked familiar.

Intrigued, Alex clicked on one of the reference pages, one called *The History of Bishops Hill*. It was an old, self-made website with a plain black background and yellow text in Comic Sans font. It even had some basic, archaic animations dotted around that made the site look extremely cheesy. However, there was a section in the side bar that he clicked on, one that focused on a very particular area of Bishops Hill.

An area that was apparently known as Dunton Farm. He read the article.

His gut feeling was confirmed.

It turns out the farm on this land that his mother had inherited—which she had mentioned earlier—was called Dunton Farm, the mill that still stood being the only remnant of it. The page said the farm had been owned by the Dunton family, who were quite wealthy and well-regarded in the area. It then went on to tell of Thomas Kerr, a teenage farm-hand who was apparently unusually large for his age. In addition to that, it seemed he also had severe learning difficulties—though the description on the page was much less kind.

It outlined the story pretty much as Wikipedia had, though there were some extra bits added; a little more in the way of legend and lore.

The murders took place in the year 1679, when the parents of the family left their three children alone at home to attend a gathering of friends, taking a horse and cart farther into town. The Wikipedia page told, in a straightforward manner, how Kerr, who was well-known to the Dunton children—and usually teased by the middle child—killed each of them in turn with an axe.

It also described his conviction and execution: placed in a gibbet cage, suspended from a tall post and left to die and rot. His body on show for the people of the town to see.

This website, however, was put together by a local man who had access to historical records of the event, or so he claimed. He went into detail of how Thomas Kerr heard a voice that night, a voice that insisted he kill the children.

A voice he obeyed.

Grabbing an axe, he chased them around the house. They fled from him, screaming for their lives, and ran into a bedroom.

Once inside, they tried to barricade the door. Kerr, however, set to work on it with the axe, chopping and wearing down the door's integrity. As he was about to get through, the eldest child, Alice—supposedly a golden-haired girl of fifteen—threw herself against the door to try to block his entry. The axe again came down, splintering more wood. As it finished its swing, it buried itself into her arm at the wrist, lopping off her hand.

Kerr then forced his way inside and threw Alice to the ground. The middle child, Andrew, attacked Thomas, but was easily overpowered. Kerr struck him with the handle of the axe, supposedly giving off a sickening crack as the wood connected with his skull, fracturing it. The large teenager then got to work on the two prone children, hacking at their bodies, paying specific attention to their heads and neck until whatever was left was unrecognisable.

Then he turned his attention to the youngest, Ellie, who was hiding under a bed. She begged and pleaded for her life.

According to what was written, Ellie and Thomas Kerr were actually friendly with each other prior to that night.

This friendship, and her pleading, seemed to snap the young man from his trance.

He began to walk away from his terrible deed, however something appeared before him.

Alex had to read this part twice.

A monster.

A horrible, inhuman thing.

Thomas Kerr assumed it to be the Devil himself.

And, it seemed, the Devil was not about to let Thomas Kerr end the bloodletting just yet. It spoke.

Go back, thou hateful wretch, resume thy cursed knife. I long to view more blood, spare not the young one's life.

And, again, Thomas Kerr obeyed.

Poor little Ellie Dunton was slain.

The parents returned home later that evening and found Kerr outside, sitting on a log. He was covered in blood and mumbling incoherently to himself. The parents instantly knew something was wrong, and when the mother confronted Thomas, he simply said he'd done what he had to in order to save his soul.

The parents then found their children.

The authorities were summoned and Kerr went along without resistance, showing remorse only for the death of little Ellie.

He was quickly tried and executed, living out his final days trapped in a metal cage on show for all to see who cared to look. He suffered from starvation, exposure, and even the ceaselessly pecking beaks of the crows that feasted on his flesh.

The bodies of the children were laid to rest at St. Peters church in Bishops Hill. The website also said that, supposedly, the remains of Thomas Kerr were also put to rest in the same cemetery in an unmarked grave.

These weren't the only murders to take place at the site, either. After the Kerr murders, the farm cycled through a number of owners until it became abandoned, left to rot and ruin. Then, starting in 1866, a number of people in the area began to go missing. It wasn't until the abandoned farm was fully searched over a year later that locals found a most horrific sight. Bodies in all stages of decomposition, hidden in the attic. A local woman named Margaret Hobbes was hiding out in there, alive and well.

Upon further questioning, she said that she had been forced from her home. She had run from an abusive spouse and took shelter in the only place she could find. Then, once at the farm, she swore she had begun to see and hear strange things. Things that got into her head and made sinister promises in exchange for her soul.

And she obeyed.

She would lure men back with promises of sex and poison them with arsenic. But the bodies found were not all adults. She eventually confessed to kidnapping children, too, and murdering them, but not just with poison. Some of the killings were much more... intimate.

All, apparently, at the command of a demonic presence she had encountered at the farm.

The townspeople that found her were enraged and—overcome by mob-mentality—set fire to the buildings, all that would take hold, and scorched them from the earth.

It was said the mill would not burn, but with the other buildings all satisfactorily ablaze the mob felt their work was done.

Margaret Hobbes was hanged in 1867.

The site remained abandoned until bought by an out-of-towner in the early 1900s. He built again on the plot, but didn't remain there long, and it changed hands many times over the years, though records of this were not available on the website.

Alex let himself sink further into his sofa. All of that was simply superstition, of course. Stories told to excuse violent and evil acts. That much he was certain of.

There was no such thing as demons.

His father had to be right about that.

But even so, knowing the land that his mother grew up on had such a tainted history was surprising, to say the very least. He wondered if his mother knew about this sordid past.

Alex scrolled farther down the page to see scans of old pictures at the bottom. Some were of the original buildings, some of the aftermath of the fire.

And there was one of Margaret Hobbes.

Upon seeing it, his blood ran cold.

15

DANNI'S TEARS WERE SPENT.

After the fight she knew she had to get away from Jon before things escalated any further. She had stormed off and, though she didn't know why, headed to her father's old room. She slammed the door behind her, sat on the bed, and wept.

She allowed herself a few minutes to cry; purging her body of the built-up tension, anger, and regret, then forced herself to stop. Danni knew she couldn't just hide up here all night. It would just prove Jon right, that she was running away from adversity again, and she did not want to give him that satisfaction.

The fight downstairs had shocked her. He had never been like that with her before.

Ever.

The thread he was pulling at, and the apparent glee with which he pulled, wasn't like him. Jon knew it was a deeply troubling subject for her, yet he unloaded on her with both barrels.

She had been no better. When she had him on the

ropes, unleashing her own set of truths, she could see her words cutting him deeply.

And in amongst the anger, that felt good.

What had brought them to this point?

The stress of the weekend was a possibility. However, she'd never envisioned that of all the difficulties they would face during their stay, this would be one of them. She'd just assumed that Jon's unwavering strength and support would have been guaranteed.

And that proved not to be the case.

It wasn't like him.

It was like he was different here.

One thing Danni did know, however, was that they couldn't just leave things like this. They needed to talk more and make sure it didn't veer off into another argument. And, while she was owed a hell of a fucking apology for how he had talked to her, she needed to put things right. She wasn't the only one suffering this weekend, and it was doing the children no good seeing them at each other like this.

She looked around the room to see it was basically as she remembered. Sparse, dusty, and devoid of any warmth. A nightstand was next to the bed, and on it sat an old lamp and several large bottles of golden liquid. She unscrewed the top of one of them and took a sniff of the pungent alcohol inside.

Scotch.

It was her father's favourite drink, and drinking always made him worse, made him angrier. There was a small metal bin close to the bed that was full of empty bottles. Danni realised his drinking must have actually gotten worse after she'd fled.

A large wardrobe dominated the wall opposite the old four-poster bed, and a matching dresser hugged the adjacent wall that separated the room from the hallway outside. Opposite that, a double-length window overlooked the front of the property. From here, she could see the road outside and the stretch of fields beyond that. Fields that were, at first, faded and yellowed, and progressed to sharper greens the farther out they got.

The rest of the room was littered with clothing piled on the floor in no kind of order, and Danni had no idea if they were clean or not. She knew that many years ago, when she was very, very young, this room had been different. Another hand had arranged and decorated it, and it had been a happier place.

For a time.

Until her mother took her own life.

Then the darkness came.

The cold.

She stood and walked carefully around the room, looking at the nightstand and the top of the dresser. There were no pictures anywhere. Not of her, or her mother. Old Arthur obviously had no desire to remember either of them.

She pulled open the top dresser drawer, curious to discover if this really was the case, or if, as she hoped, he had memories of them hidden somewhere.

Anything to prove that her father, her own flesh and blood, maybe wasn't the absolute monster she remembered.

Surely there was some good in those old bones before he died?

The first drawer revealed only clothes. Not folded, simply shoved in. The second showed the same, and the third was empty.

That left only the bottom drawer.

She expected it to be empty, too, just like the last, but as she opened it a single object slid into view. It was a worn-looking notebook with a ring binder to one side. The light-brown, leather cover was creased. She picked it up and opened it to the first page to see that it was filled with well-written handwriting.

And a date at the top.

3rd February, 1984

Today was a good day. So good, in fact, that it pushed me to start something I've always wanted to. A diary. Alice gave me the news today. She is pregnant. We are going to have a baby. It's hard to put into words just how happy this makes me. Those that have children will know the feeling all too well. It is happiness like I have never known before. Marrying Alice was the best day of my life, but I know now that soon that day will have stiff competition. I plan to keep this diary going, and to write in it constantly, both as a way to chronicle my journey towards, and through, fatherhood, but also as something to leave to my soon-to-be child. It may not be much, and I hereby strive to provide everything the child will need in life, but perhaps this journal will mean more than other material possessions.

I don't know, maybe these are just the ramblings of a soppy, love-struck old fool. But I don't believe they are. I want this to be a special document.

My child, I hope that if one day you ever read this, it brings you even a small amount of the happiness that I know you will bring me.

Danni realised she was crying again.

This was her father's diary, but the words, and the feeling with which they were written, seemed alien to her. It was not the same man she knew.

She read on, learning about her parents' excitement at her upcoming arrival. She even learned they had a scare, a bleed, and saw the anguish and worry her father went through.

It cannot be fair to give someone this kind of hope, only to snatch it away. I spoke with Peter Atkins about this, and he simply said it is out of our hands and God will look after us. What kind of God would enjoy this sort of cruel abuse? I want to help my wife, to comfort her, but I don't know how to do that.

It's the waiting.

No quick answers, no explanations, just the knowledge that everything might be fine... or it might not. But we have to wait to find out.

And there is nothing to do while you wait, either. Just worry. You can try to busy your mind, but the fear is always there. Buried in my gut.

The knowledge that this poor, unborn child may never get a chance at life is more than I can bear.

Danni learned that the bleeding subsided, and they saw out the rest of the pregnancy with no further concerns. But she'd had no idea that it had ever happened. Then, flicking ahead, she read the entry about her birth, written a few days after she had come into this world.

I don't really know how to put this into words.

My daughter, Danielle Watson, arrived only two days ago. She is all I can think about.

There are moments in life you know will be special. But knowing this and experiencing it are two vastly different things.

I smile as I write this, but in many respects she was an ugly little thing: a wrinkly, grey, pudgy baby. The way all babies are. But, she was also the most beautiful thing in the world.

And holding her in my arms for the very first time...

I could never do that experience justice with the written word. So, I won't begin to try.

Just know, Danielle, if you ever read this, you made me happier than I thought possible.

Danni was reeling.

Reading these words, feeling her father's emotion and the love he had for her made her wonder what had happened to turn him into the monster he had become. She almost wanted to stop, just leave it there and take comfort in the knowledge that, at one time, he was a seemingly kind, loving man.

But she turned the page and read on, skimming until she read of their move to a larger house.

The mid-terraced property they were in was just too small for them, and apparently her father had earned himself a good promotion.

It would have been a stretch, financially, to afford this place. Thankfully, it comes with a past; one that has harmed its selling value. Other people's superstition has become my good fortune. It is perfect for our needs: big enough so that we can add to the family one day, and it gives us a good deal of privacy. It even has an old mill on the edge of the property, one that I fancy we could fix up and convert into a nice living space for us.

This place could be perfect. Sometimes, I cannot believe my luck in life.

Danni learned that they moved in, and that the first few months were happy.

But then, things began to change.

I know how this will sound, but I fear something is wrong with Alice. She is becoming sharp with me. And with Danielle, too. It worries me. I know she is not sleeping. Last night I awoke and found her sitting up in bed, watching me. I wish I could say she was smiling, just happily gazing at me as I slept, but the look on her face was not one of love, nor of kindness.

The diary went on, growing progressively worse.

Alice often goes out to the mill alone. Says she likes the privacy and peace out there. Danielle is far from a needy child, and I try to give my wife space when she feels like this, so why does she need to go there for some kind of peace? On top of that, there is nothing in that mill; it's empty, dark and dirty.

And yet she still prefers to go out there, alone, rather than spend much time with us. I try, but still she pulls away from me.

With her acting like this, the house, our home, has a darker, colder feel to it. We are not the family I wanted us to be.

I just want to know what I need to do, so that I can fix this for her.

Worse, and I know how this sounds, I always feel like I'm being watched in this damn house. It seems unsafe, somehow, and I worry for my child.

I fear I am struggling to cope.

Then, another entry:

Alice was in tears tonight. She said there is something here, something that talks to her and eats away at her mind. She wasn't making much sense, but her words scared me. She told me how this thing wanted to control her, and to have her act out its will. To cause pain.

I asked her what she meant, and who was she supposed to cause pain to.

Her answer?

Me.

And Danielle.

I exploded in anger, I'm ashamed to say. I yelled and screamed, telling her I didn't know what was wrong, but she couldn't say things like that about our daughter. I think I even threatened to have her committed. It wasn't the help a troubled mind needed, but I couldn't control myself.

As Danni read on, she followed the deterioration of her mother's mental state until finally it all came to a head.

It has been over a week since it happened.

I have long since given up hope of this diary being a gift to my daughter. I now cling to it as a place to unburden myself, to help keep my sanity. Something I will need over the coming months, I fear.

Alice is dead.

Last Monday, she was not next to me in bed when I awoke. This wasn't strange in and of itself, but she was not in the house either. I figured she'd be out in that damn mill again.

Turns out I was right.

I opened the door and stepped inside. The morning light gave some illumination to the almost unnatural dark of the place. Alice was hanging before me.

A thin rope tied to a timber strut above cut into her neck as she swayed gently from side to side. I remember her glassy eyes, how they almost popped from her bloated face.

There was a note on the floor, messily written. I transcribe it here, so that I never forget:

I'm sorry, Arthur. This is what I have to do to protect you and my daughter. Doing so has taken the last of my strength, but I won't let that thing take me. You and Danielle must leave this place. Know that I love you, and that what I became in the end was not really me.

Alice.

And that was the note, in full.

Danielle was devastated by her mother's death, as any young girl would be. I, too, am crushed. My heart is ripped out, and it feels like I have been physically punched and I cannot get my breath.

The funeral was horrendous.

The weather was pleasant, and there was a most generous turnout, but it was the single most difficult day of my life. Being there for poor Danielle is so hard when I'm crumbling inside myself.

What will we do now?

Danni set the book down.

She had no idea.

Danni had always thought, assumed, that her mother had taken her own life due to being unhappy, given what kind of man Arthur was.

But the story about her mother, what she went through, what she thought she was fighting in the house, scared Danni. Too many strange happenings were linked to this place for it to be some kind of coincidence. She remembered her father's words in the diary, saying that it had come with some kind of a past. She also recalled when her friends from school playfully teased her for living in a spook house. Danni knew bad things had happened on the land—she'd always known that, it was normal for her. But other than what had happened in the past, she assumed everything else was just legend and scary stories.

No different than every other small town in England.

Growing up, she had paid it no real mind.

So, could there actually be more to it?

Again, Danni began to read, hopeful to get some insight into her father's state of mind. To find out how he went from a seemingly loving man to what he eventually became.

She was not disappointed.

Certain snippets began to worm their way into his writing like an infestation.

It's so hard.

Alice has taken the easy way out and left the burden to me. Sometimes I have thoughts that shame me, but they persist.

In another passage:

That damn child is pushing me past my breaking point. Why can't she just do as she's told?

And more:

She's like her mother. Same cowardly type of woman. I would not be surprised to find that her mother's spirit has somehow taken hold in the girl, in an effort to torment me and make me suffer.

They are all the same.

Snakes with breasts.

Nothing more.

Danni was horrified. But the writing became ever more hateful.

Yelling at the girl gets a good enough response. I push it as far as I can, just to see the fear in her. It's enjoyable.

Just as that thing said it would be.

A horrible, inhuman, terrifying thing it may be, but it seems to speak the truth. Perhaps I should listen to it more.

Danni's stomach tightened.

Such a release. My father always drilled into me that striking a girl was as cowardly and despicable an act as could be conceived. I laugh when I think how he would have reacted seeing me strike a young girl.

More and more she read, and the writing veered into violent scribbles, becoming messier and harder to decipher.

It seems that striking the bitch is not enough. I know she is scared, but her fear hasn't yet reached its peak. The thing in the mill wants more, and I need to provide it. I know what I must do. If others ever find out, I will be shunned, hated, and arrested. So be it. My soul is claimed, so there is nothing that can be done to me now that I cannot bear. She is of age, anyway. I'll do it tonight.

Danni flipped through even further.

It is done. The thing is pleased. I don't know how I feel, but I know I must keep going. Only one thing left now. I need to take my daughter's life.

Danni realised, in horror, just how much of a lucky escape she'd had when she had run away all those years ago. She had no idea what he'd really been planning.

That fucking bitch has escaped! Ran off and left me. No matter where I look or who I call, I can't find her!

The fucking cunt.

She has ruined my plans. Selfish, loathsome bitch! If I ever see her again, I'll wrap my hands around her little throat and not stop squeezing until the life drains from her eyes.

The rest of the journal was filled with more hateful bile. It stopped being a diary and instead turned into random thoughts of cruelty and hate. Most of it directed at Danni. She saw a section focusing on Annie—the girl from the funeral—and how her father was furious at her for escaping as well.

Just how close had he come to killing someone?

Thankfully, the pages ran dry. The rest of the book was empty.

All except the last page.

I cannot fight this.

I'm sorry.

Please forgive me.

Danni let the book fall to the floor and swayed on her feet, unable to process what she had just read.

It was all too much. Seeing once-loving parents turned into such monsters.

And by what?

Something that didn't seem possible. Her head continued to swim, and the room began to blur.

She was faintly aware that she was passing out.

As she fell, and darkness claimed her, she swore she could see a figure watching her from the corner of the room.

Dad?

16

Jon found Danni in her father's old bedroom.

She had been upstairs too long, so, growing impatient, he had gone up to look for her and found her sprawled out on the floor. The shock of seeing her this way caused a surge of panic in him, and his heart raced. He instinctively ran to his wife and gently shook her, bringing her back to consciousness.

'Danni,' he said, shaking her again as her eyes began to focus. 'Are you okay?'

He helped her to a sitting position and saw that she had dark circles under her eyes and looked tired.

'What the hell happened?' he asked, noticing the small notebook on the floor next to her.

'I don't know,' Danni said, rubbing her forehead. 'I must have passed out.' She then looked around and her eyes widened. 'It's getting dark, how long have I been up here?'

'Hours,' Jon said, putting a hand on her shoulder. 'I wanted to give you space, but started to get worried. Then I found you like this...'

'I'm okay,' she said, still looking a little dazed.

'Okay? Since when have you been in the habit of fainting?'

Danni shrugged. 'I don't know. Everything must have just gotten to me.'

She looked down, then picked up the notebook. She ran a finger across its cover.

'What's that?' Jon asked.

'Something I found,' Danni said. 'It was my father's.'

'And what's in it?'

Danni shrugged. 'Just stuff.'

She was being evasive, and it didn't sit well with Jon. He felt a small pang of agitation pierce his concern. He didn't want another argument, though. He just wanted to get through the night.

'Let's get you downstairs,' Jon said. He hooked an arm around her waist and helped her to her feet, giving her a moment to get her balance before releasing her. 'You sure you're okay?' he asked.

She nodded, still holding the book. 'Yeah.'

Something still hung in the air between them, a sense of unfinished business. Jon still remembered the sting of that slap she'd given him earlier.

And she owed him an apology for that.

Then, as if on cue, 'I'm sorry for hitting you earlier,' she said, without making eye contact.

'Thank you,' he said. 'I didn't want to argue, and we shouldn't have done it with the kids around. I know this is tough for you, and I shouldn't have pushed you so hard.'

He stopped short of actually saying sorry, thinking it was probably implicit in his words. Besides, did he really have anything to apologise for? He was only speaking the truth.

Danni frowned at him, apparently unsatisfied with what he'd offered. But it was all she was getting.

'Come on,' he said and rubbed her arm. 'Let's go downstairs. We need to figure out what we are doing for food.'

He knew she was going to say something, and he also knew it was to press things again, which would probably lead to another fight. To be frank, he didn't have the patience for it, so he walked from the room and headed back downstairs, drawing the exchange to a close.

Danni was left dumbfounded.

Was that his attempt at an apology? She'd swallowed her pride in an effort to make amends, but all he'd managed was to outline what had gone wrong, as if that was lost on her. Then he had decided that food was more important and marched off like they were done.

What the hell had come over him?

It wasn't the Jon she knew.

She looked again at the diary, still haunted by what she'd read. It was a struggle—given how impossible it all was— but she was fast coming to terms with the fact that something was very wrong with this house.

And she needed to get her family away from it.

Now.

That would invariably lead to another fight with Jon, especially considering the late hour. It was almost fully dark outside now, which meant travelling at night, and that wouldn't help her case.

It was only after she'd taken her first step towards the door that Danni remembered the last thing she'd seen before blacking out.

Her father, peeking from the shadows with dark eyes and a black smile.

Being upstairs on her own suddenly made her feel very vulnerable. Goosebumps formed on her forearms. She hugged the diary close to her chest and strode from the room, flicking off the light as she went. She walked quickly to the top of the stairs... and stopped.

Her body tensed.

Danni was certain she had heard a whisper.

She slowly turned around, but saw no one behind her. Then she flicked her eyes up towards the attic hatch.

It was open, revealing the attic above.

And standing just on the edge of the hatch, looking down at her, was a man.

He was tall and bare chested, with horrible marks and scratches on his grey body. Small chunks of skin were missing in places, revealing blackened flesh beneath.

His mouth hung open at a disjointed angle, and a long tongue writhed and moved, snakelike, with a life of its own.

The corners of his mouth pulled up a little, giving the hint of a smile.

Danni screamed and ran down the stairs, taking them as quickly as she could. She worried she was going too fast, that her momentum would make her lose her footing and send her sprawling uncontrollably to the bottom. And, a little over halfway down the descent, that is exactly what happened.

She missed her footing on one stair, twisted her ankle, and her body toppled forward. Her hip crashed into the edge of a step, and she yelped at the sharp explosion of pain. The only thing she could think to do as she fell was to make her body go limp while she tumbled the rest of the way down.

'Mom!' she heard a voice yell from the living room. Danni was on her side, dazed and in pain. She saw her daughter looking through from the other room with a shocked and worried expression on her face.

Danni wanted to tell her not to worry, that she was fine, but she didn't know if that was true or not. Her body was wracked with pain, and she was barely able to get her bearings. She managed to roll onto her back, now aware that Jon had come into the hallway.

Whilst on her back, she looked up the length of the stairs to the attic hatch. It was still open, but the man she had seen was no longer there.

'Jesus,' Jon said, kneeling by her side. 'Are you okay?'

He sounded genuinely worried, which slightly surprised Danni, given how he'd been acting.

'I think so,' she eventually said. Her ankle screamed in disagreement, as did her hip, but she knew things could have been much worse.

'What happened?'

She was about to tell him what she had seen, what had caused her to run down the stairs and fall, but stopped herself. She knew he wouldn't believe it.

'I fell,' she said, as if it were the most obvious thing in the world. Leah emerged from the living room, followed by Alex.

'What about the scream?' he asked.

Danni paused. 'I lost my footing at the top,' she lied, trying to repress the ever-growing fear building up in her. 'I must have screamed when I started to fall.'

There *was* something in this house.

'Jesus,' Jon said, helping her up as he had in her father's bedroom only minutes ago. Danni made sure to grab the notebook as she got to her feet. 'Sounds like you took a hell of a tumble. You sure you're okay?'

'I'm sure,' she said again, holding her side. Without

thinking, she tried to put weight on her right ankle and cried out as a jolt of pain spread from the injured joint.

'You're hurt,' he said, ducking under the arm she was resting on the bannister, letting her settle her weight on him.

'I think I've twisted my ankle.'

'Come on, let's get you to the sofa. We need to get you off your feet.'

She wanted to protest, but he was already leading her through to the living room. Jon carefully lowered her down into the seat and helped her swing her legs up.

I don't want to get off my feet. I want to get the hell out of here.

'Stay there,' Jon said, 'I'll go and fix you a drink. Do you want something to help with the pain? I'm sure we packed paracetamol.'

'Shouldn't we take her to an emergency room?' Leah asked. 'We need to get her ankle checked out. She's hurt.'

The idea was a welcome one, a perfect excuse to get them all out of here, at least for a few hours.

'That might not be a bad idea,' Danni said.

'Nonsense,' Jon said, getting to his feet. 'I took a fall, too, and I'm fine. I'll get you a nice, big glass of red and some pain killers. Just keep your leg elevated, and by morning you'll be as good as new.'

He then left the room.

Something was wrong with this.

Very wrong.

'Dad really doesn't want to leave this place, huh?' Leah asked her.

'I guess not,' Danni said, trying not to convey the concern she was feeling.

'What's that?' Alex asked, pointing to the book.

'Just something I found upstairs,' Danni said.

'What's in it?'

'Nothing too interesting, I'm sure.' She tucked the book beside her, between her thigh and the back of the sofa.

'Should we phone an ambulance?' Leah asked.

'But Dad said—'

Leah cut Alex off, apparently not interested in hearing what her father had said. 'I don't care. Mom's hurt.'

'I'm fine,' Danni said, not fully convinced herself. The physical injuries appeared to be minor, but she could still picture that man looking down at her from the attic. She wondered if it was the same person Leah had seen up in the bathroom the previous night. Part of her wanted to ask the question, to help confirm her suspicions, but she was more focused on protecting her daughter, not scaring her any further.

Jon soon returned with a large glass of red wine. He handed it to Danni, along with a small pack of painkillers.

'Should she be mixing those?' Leah asked.

Jon gave a dismissive wave of the hand. 'She'll be fine. It's only paracetamol.' He then clapped his hands together. 'Okay, I'm going to order us some pizza.'

'Again?' Alex asked. 'I didn't think you were a fan of pizza, Dad.'

'Well, I don't think there's much to choose from around here, so I figure we should make the best of it. Or does anyone want to try something different?'

'Pizza is fine for me,' Danni said, taking a tentative sip of her wine. That small sip turned into a larger, self-indulgent gulp. It tasted good and was warm as it hit her stomach. Her mind was still working overtime on how to get through to Jon, and how to get them out of here. Perhaps alcohol wasn't really a good choice to help with that.

'And me,' Leah said in a low voice.

'Alex?' Jon asked, turning to his son.

'Yeah, same again for me, I guess.'

'Excellent,' he said and walked from the room, reappearing shortly after with the menu they'd used the previous night. 'I'm just going to nip outside to order, hopefully I can get a signal out there. Anyone changed their minds and want to order something a bit more adventurous?'

From Danni's perspective on the sofa, she could see a tiny sliver of his body through the crack of the door-jamb. She saw movement and was certain he was tucking something into his pocket. She couldn't be sure, but it looked to be the keys to the SUV.

His question was met with silence from everyone. 'Suit yourselves,' he said and went outside.

To say Danni was confused at Jon's behaviour was an understatement. He seemed oddly upbeat, in a way that was almost forced. It made Danni uneasy. How could he be so chipper after seeing his wife take such a fall only moments earlier? Throw in the fight they'd had with each other as well, and his demeanour was downright odd.

'What's up with him?' Leah asked, obviously in tune with Danni's concern.

'I have no idea,' Danni said.

They could hear him outside through the thin windows placing the order. Once finished, Danni saw him walk by the front window to the side of the house.

'Where's he going?' Danni asked. Leah walked to the window and looked out. 'Not sure, he's out of view. Around the back, I think. Should I go check?'

Danni thought about it. 'Go to the dining room and look out there, see if you can see him. Alex, you go too.'

The two children obeyed, and Danni could hear the *click, click, click* of Alex's crutches as he went. She waited, keen to see what he was up to. 'What's he doing?' she called to the pair.

'It looks like he's going over to the mill,' Alex yelled back.

'The door's open,' Leah added. 'Was it open before?'

A tight, anxious feeling squeezed in Danni's chest. Then she heard Leah scream.

'What the fuck is that?' the girl cried.

17

ALEX WAS STRUGGLING to make sense of what he was seeing.

At first he was confused as to why his father was heading towards that old mill. The door to the building was open, so perhaps he had gone over to close it?

But then, Alex saw something reveal itself from the darkness. Something he couldn't understand.

An impossibility.

He wanted to yell for his mother as Leah started to scream again.

Whatever the thing was, it was tall—stooping down to be seen through the doorway—and spindly, with elongated features. Even at this distance, however, he could see that it simply wasn't human. Its face was... terrifying, with a mass of eyes over its large, brain-like cranium, and a vertical mouth that slowly opened and closed, as if tasting the air.

And yet, Alex's father continued walking. There was no way he could have missed the abomination in the doorway, but he simply strode onward towards the mill. He stepped inside, and the door slowly closed.

Alex continued to focus on the mill, unable to look away

as he heard movement from the hallway behind. And his focus changed, drawn to something he noticed in the reflection of the glass door. Directly behind him, Alex saw a figure. At first, he assumed it to be his mother.

But it was wearing black, and it was too close. He saw the blurred face in the reflection pull a blackened smile.

Alex spun around with a gasp, but there was no one there. He heard someone approaching from the hallway, saw his mother limp into view. His heart hammered in his chest.

What was going on?

'What is it?' his mother asked, her eyes wide.

'Over there,' Leah answered, her voice shaking as she pointed to the dark mill outside. 'Something was in there.'

'And Dad's gone in,' Alex added.

He realised that his breathing was becoming quicker and quicker. The reflection had been of the same old woman he'd seen upstairs yesterday, he was sure of it. And that had been the same woman he'd seen on the website earlier today: Margaret Hobbes.

It couldn't be real. On some level, he knew that. And he knew how disappointed his father would be to find out he had been entertaining thoughts to the contrary.

But he couldn't help it.

Alex had never heard of Margaret Hobbes before today, let alone seen a picture of her. And yet, he had seen her. Yesterday, up in the bedroom—it was her, of that there was no question. The old woman looked exactly like she had in the picture he saw a day later, if a little more twisted.

On top of that, there was Leah's experience in the shower.

This wasn't just a case of them scaring themselves. They had both witnessed inhuman things.

That couldn't be explained away, could it?

'What do you mean?' his mother asked, hopping closer to them, careful to avoid putting too much weight on her bad ankle. She looked out through the door. 'What was in the mill? What did you see?' Her words came out fast and panicked.

'I... I don't know,' Alex said. 'I can't describe it.'

'It was a monster,' Leah said. 'And Dad just walked inside with it, like it wasn't even there.'

'Mom,' Alex said. 'Dad's in danger. He's in there with that thing.'

His mother looked to him, and he could see the fear in her eyes. He hadn't expected her to believe what they had told her, so outlandish was the story, but that didn't seem to be the case.

'What's going on, Mom?' Leah asked.

'I'm not sure,' she replied. 'But we need to get out of here.'

'What about Dad?' Alex asked. 'We can't just leave him.'

'I know,' his mother said, 'and we won't, but right now we need to move. I need to get you two out of here. Everyone head to the car.'

'Mom?' Alex wanted to argue further. He was concerned she was thinking of leaving his father behind.

'Now!' she snapped. She grabbed them both and ushered them into the hallway, limping along behind.

Alex's mother pushed him along quickly, but he was struggling to maintain the speed she wanted him to achieve. He worked his crutches as quickly as he could, but was worried he would lose his footing.

Once in the hallway, they stopped in their tracks as all the lights blinked out.

The waning light of dusk seeped in from the single

glazed panel in the front door, and it allowed them to see the figure standing directly in front of them, blocking their exit.

Not the old woman this time.

This was a man. An old man with broad shoulders and a rotund stomach. He stood stock still, arms by his side, eyes lost in pools of black shadows.

His thin mouth spread open into a menacing smile, revealing stained teeth and dark, purple gums.

Alex shrieked in fear.

Then his mother uttered something in a shocked voice that scared him further.

'Dad?'

The old man's smile did not change at all. He was motionless, like a twisted, grinning painting, and yet they all heard a malevolent laugh ring out around them.

'What do we do?' Leah asked in a quivering voice.

Before Leah could get an answer, they heard another laugh echo from behind, this one higher in pitch. More feminine.

But no less insidious.

All three instinctively pressed themselves together, huddling tight, and turned around to see the same old woman Alex had seen before. She was standing right behind them in the doorway to the kitchen, blocking the way back.

Margaret Hobbes.

Leah screamed, and Alex felt like crying. He didn't know what to do.

His mother grabbed their hands and pulled them towards the living room door, but they soon found that route was cut off as well.

A tall man, with pale skin and horrible wounds on his

body, ducked through the doorway. His jaw was loose, swinging as he moved.

Thomas Kerr.

Alex clung to his mother as tightly as he could, unable to process what was happening. The fear was debilitating.

He felt a warmth spread from his crotch as his bladder emptied.

'What do we do?' Leah asked, sobbing.

'Stay away from us,' Alex heard his mother say through gritted teeth. 'Just stay the fuck away.'

The laughter continued from both the old woman and what appeared to be Alex's grandfather. They were both still motionless, but the tall man with the open wounds covering his body continued to stumble towards them.

Alex felt himself pulled sideways as his mother dragged both he and Leah around the banister and onto the stairs. As Alex passed before the grinning old man he felt an intense cold, like a blast from a refrigerator.

'Come on,' his mother urged, shoving them both up the stairs as quickly as they could go. But they were moving too fast, and Alex's legs began to ache.

'Mom,' he said, trying to get his breath as they turned at the landing and thundered along the hallway.

'Keep going,' she said, guiding them to the spare bedroom which was directly above the living room.

'I'm scared,' Leah said, openly crying now. She squatted down and wrapped her arms around herself.

'No,' their mother said, pulling Leah back to her feet. 'We need to keep moving.'

'Where?' Alex asked, wanting to break down in tears himself. His mother had already moved over to the window and was fighting with the handle.

She had to be kidding.

The window's bottom section swung outwards, enough for them to fit through. 'Come on,' his mother urged, frantic.

'Out the window?' Alex asked. 'It's too high.'

'It's not,' she replied. 'The bay window to the living room is right below us. It's not that far down, we just drop onto the roof of the window and then down to the ground.'

'What if we fall?'

'We won't fall,' she said, her voice rising. 'Now come on, both of you, we need to move.'

Neither Alex nor his sister reacted, so Danni stomped over and pulled Leah to the window.

'I can't,' Leah cried.

'You can.'

Leah wanted to argue more, but was pushed, as carefully as possible, to the window frame. Alex watched as his sister leaned her head out and looked down. She immediately drew it back in.

'It's too high,' she said.

'It's not. You need to do this, Leah, we can't stay here. Now come on, honey, just be brave for me.'

'I'm scared.'

'I know you are, but you know we have to go. We can't stay here. It'll all be fine, sweetie, I promise. Alex and I will be right behind you.'

Alex walked over to the window as well and looked out at the drop.

Leah, still crying, seemed to heed her mother's words. She began to move, painfully slowly, and stepped up onto the window sill, holding on to the jamb for dear life. She swung a leg outside.

'Now lower yourself down, Leah. Just be careful.'

Leah did as instructed. Grasping the sill, she let her body lower until she was hanging from the window.

Looking out, Alex could see her dangling feet were still a foot from the flat roof of the bay window below.

'I can't let go, Mom,' Leah said.

'Yes you can, Leah. Yes you can. Just be careful.'

Alex could see the hesitation in Leah's face. But, she closed her eyes and let go.

Alex held his breath as he watched his sister drop. Her feet made contact with the roof below, and for a moment tipped to one side, desperately pinwheeling her arms to regain her balance.

Thankfully, she succeeded.

'Now wait there, don't fall,' Danni shouted and turned to Alex. 'Now you.'

He shook his head, but his mother didn't hesitate. She grabbed him and pulled him towards the opening.

'Let go of your crutches, Alex. We'll bring them down afterwards.'

'I don't think I—'

'No,' she said, cutting him off. 'We don't have time. You can do this, I know you can. Your sister is right below you, and she'll catch you. Now climb out, just like she did. I'll help you.'

Alex was resistant. He wanted a moment to get used to the idea that he was about to jump from a first-floor window, but that opportunity was not given to him. His mother forcefully guided him through the opening, and he felt the cool air from outside on his face. He gazed down and instantly felt dizzy. It looked so high from up here.

'Now lower yourself down, just like your sister did.'

His body shook, and he feared his bodyweight would be too much for his arms to bear. But he lowered himself down, feeling his mother's supporting hands from above helping to lessen his weight.

'Leah, grab hold of your brother's legs and help lower him down.'

As Alex dangled helplessly, he felt his sister grab his ankles.

'I've got you,' she said.

'Now drop,' his mother said. Alex closed his eyes as his sister had, took a breath, and let go.

He felt himself drop, weightless, until his legs made contact with the roof. He felt a flash of pain run up his shins, and he cried out, toppling backwards. Leah tried to hold him, but he stumbled into her, knocking her backwards as well.

They both fell, clutching one another, over the edge of the roof.

'No!' he heard his mother scream from above as the world around him spun. The pain from his legs was eclipsed when both he and Leah landed hard onto the concrete footpath below.

Alex hit his head, and pinpricks of light danced before his eyes. He rolled onto his back and exhaled as he felt his sister untangle herself from him.

'Alex, are you okay?' he heard her say. He looked past her to see the horrified face of his mother above as she leaned from the open window.

'Mom!' he yelled back, terrified.

The grinning old man was standing directly behind her.

18

JON HADN'T PHONED in a pizza.

Instead, he'd simply put on a show, as he knew his family would be listening.

Danni was desperate to leave, that much was clear. And with her stupidly falling down the stairs, there had been talk about calling an ambulance.

Why couldn't they just see the truth?

They were all scared of nothing. Spooked by shadows.

If he got them to stay and face their fears, then they would see that he was right; that there was nothing to be afraid of.

Running away would solve nothing, so he had to stop that from happening. And to do that, he needed time to think.

The night was drawing in rapidly, and though the temperature was dropping outside, the sting of the cold was refreshing. The air itself seemed different in this part of the world; cleaner, more pure.

He liked it.

Better than the smog-infested pollution that they all had

to breathe in London on a daily basis. Maybe they would be better off relocating here?

After making the fake telephone call, he had looked over to the mill and noticed the door was open.

The building intrigued him and he realised that, despite having been here for a day and a half, he hadn't even looked inside.

His curiosity was piqued, and he decided to investigate it now. He didn't want to go back inside just yet, and the privacy would give him time to think.

As he walked over to the mill he noticed something in the doorway.

Something unimaginable.

Hideous.

Not of this world.

Something demonic and evil.

He laughed to himself and kept on going.

Maybe the wild imagination of his family was contagious. He knew there was nothing there—it was all in his head, and he would not be scared by make-believe.

It beckoned him with a long, boney finger and as he approached the door, it backed off, giving him space to enter.

It would be a lie to say he wasn't scared. Part of him was terrified. And, somewhere inside of him, he heard a weak and frightened voice urging him to run. That voice was, thankfully, drowned out by reason.

There was nothing to be scared of and certainly no need to run.

He stepped inside and the door closed behind him, clicking into place and cutting off all light, save for a sliver around the edges of the door.

Strange that it had closed on its own, but no matter.

Despite the cold and dark, Jon felt oddly at peace in here. The place had a calming effect and was an escape from the constant nagging and insanity of his family. A place to quiet his mind.

He heard a voice.

It was a horrible sound, like glass scrapping down a chalkboard.

It wasn't real, though. He knew he was imagining the thing that he'd seen in the doorway speaking to him, but the vile demon seemed to make sense.

So he listened.

It told him that if his family left this place, they would never understand what it was to stand up for themselves. His children would inherit their mother's failings and forever run from adversity.

They would be weak.

Like her.

It said that they needed to stay here so they could learn a valuable lesson. At least for the night, if not longer.

The more it spoke, the more Jon understood. Danni now owned this house, so why sell it? It was a much better place to raise a family than a city. It was secluded, private, with plenty of land surrounding it, and here they had room to grow, to breathe, instead of being crammed shoulder to shoulder with strangers like they were back home.

It all made sense.

But would his family see it that way?

That was the question.

The thing in the mill gave him his answer, and it was so blindingly obvious that he felt a little embarrassed at not realising it himself.

His family would not see it his way, of course.

So, he would have to get them to understand. Make them see it his way.

And, if they still resisted, he would *force* them to stay.

It was for their own good.

It was for the best.

And they would finally realise that he knew what was best for them.

That he was right.

Jon heard a commotion outside, voices from the house. He turned and held out his hand, fumbling for the door. Something gripped his wrist, ice-cold to the touch, and guided his reach to the door handle.

Run!

The voice was his own, inside of himself, but he shrugged it off. Nothing to be scared of. He grasped the handle, and the cold hand released him. He opened the door.

It did not resist.

Jon stepped outside and jogged to the front of the house. Once there, he surveyed the scene.

'Mom,' Alex yelled. The boy was lying on the ground, his sister beside him, both seemed to be in pain. Jon glanced up and saw Danni looking out of an open, upstairs window.

An old man was standing behind her with a menacing smile on his face. Another trick of the mind, no doubt.

Nothing to worry about.

Nothing at all.

What he did have to worry about, however, was the fact that his family seemed to be up to something. Acting without his approval.

Without his say-so.

And that could not stand.

Please don't be hurt.

Danni witnessed both of her children plunge from the top of the bay window to the hard ground below. It was a drop of only about seven feet, but enough to do some damage, especially to Alex.

And it was her fault.

In her desperation, she had pushed them into doing something they clearly didn't want to do. She hadn't seen an alternative, considering the unbelievable situation they were in, but that didn't change the fact that she had caused this.

However, they did seem to be moving. Leah was getting to her feet and had Alex rolled to his back.

He cried out to her.

But, Danni noticed, he didn't seem to be crying out for help, more in warning. As he did, Danni saw Jon run into view from around the corner of the house.

And, instead of seeming concerned over what was going on, he looked furious.

Something was wrong with him, she knew that. The

story from the diary, of her mother and father and how they had changed, was fresh in her mind.

Had something similar happened to Jon?

A feeling of intense cold fell over her from behind. One that overpowered even the chilly night air from outside.

She heard that laughter again, and her body froze.

Her father was behind her. She knew it, but she was too terrified to turn around. She then felt, and could smell, his rancid breath on the back of her neck. Her breath caught in her throat, and she felt him press against her from behind.

It made her skin crawl.

'*Hello... darling,*' an echoey, raspy voice said. It seemed to strain with every word, as if the act of talking was an effort. Painful, even.

Danni felt cold hands grip her arms, and her body began to tremble.

This can't be happening.

Only a day ago, Danni felt like she had unfinished business. Things to say to her father that she would never have the chance to say. And now here he was. Right behind her.

Tormenting her again in death, just as he had in life.

'Please,' she said, softly. 'Please just leave me alone. Let me go.'

The mocking laughter returned.

'*I... will... never... leave... you... alone... again.*'

Danni began to weep. Through her tears, she saw Jon move below, dragging the children to their feet. He pointed towards the front door of the house, ordering them back inside.

'*Your... family... is... ours... now. And... we... all... belong... to... it.*'

No.

She couldn't allow that.

She wouldn't just stand by and let her family be taken by whatever the hell was behind all this. As her father started to tighten his ice-cold grip on her, Danni launched herself forward, managing to break free from the phantom hold, and leapt through the opening, bouncing off the window frame as she did.

Danni flapped her arms uselessly as she fell, trying to aim her body towards the bay window roof, the same one that Alex and Leah had dropped onto, but her momentum was too much. Her feet managed to catch the edge, taking some of the speed from her fall, but the impact was hard, and she felt a new flash of pain in her already injured ankle. In the same motion, she toppled forward and fell all the way to the ground.

She hit side-first, and the wind rushed from her body. Her head bounced off of the ground, just at the point where grass met the concrete footpath. Even though the grass was softer, her head still erupted with pain.

She wanted to let out a cry, but she didn't have the breath in her to do so. Instead, a low moan escaped her.

'Mom!' Danni heard Leah call out.

'What the fuck are you doing?'

That was Jon. Not a trace of concern, only anger.

'We need to help her.'

Alex this time. Danni opened her eyes, but her vision was blurred and everything seemed to be spinning. She felt nauseous.

'Come on,' Jon said angrily. 'Get in the house. Now. I'll deal with your mother.'

'What's wrong with you?' Leah said. 'She's hurt. We need to help her.'

'And I will, just get inside.'

'No,' Leah argued, 'we're leaving. We need to take her to a hospital. Stop being so fucking weird, Dad.'

Danni's vision was slowly coming into focus, and she could make out enough to see her husband raise his hand and strike their daughter hard across the face. There was an audible, stinging slap, and Leah let out a cry before falling to her side.

'Now, back inside!' Jon screamed.

He sounded insane.

No, Danni knew, not insane.

Possessed.

She knew now that it was time to stop regarding what was clearly taking place as being impossible. If they were going to survive, she had to accept that it was real—all of it. Danni didn't understand how or why, but she didn't need to.

All she needed to do was to get her family out of here.

To safety.

As much as it hurt to do so and made her body scream in angry protest, Danni managed to get to her feet.

'Jon,' she said, trying to keep her balance as her head still spun. She hurt all over and had no idea what injuries the fall had actually caused. She was running on pure adrenaline.

'Stay out of it, Danni,' he said, pointing a threatening finger at her. 'It's your fault this shit is happening.'

'Jon,' she said again, 'just listen to yourself. Think about what you just did to your daughter.'

Leah was on the floor holding her face, looking absolutely terrified of her father. He turned his head to look at her and studied her expression. Danni saw a moment's doubt, but it was quickly thrown off when Jon shook his head.

'Stop trying to confuse me,' he said. 'We need to toughen

these kids up, Danni. They need to grow up to be strong. But you? You just enable their fear, pushing your own insecurities on them. Well, I won't have it. So we are all going to go back in the fucking house. And what's more, we may even need to extend our stay here. It's a much better environment to bring Leah and Alex up in. And there are going to be some changes, understand?'

'This isn't you talking,' Danni said. 'It isn't. Think about what you're saying, what you're doing. It's absurd.'

'There you go again,' Jon said, taking a step towards Danni. 'Always arguing and trying to run away. If you'd just do as you're told, then you wouldn't be in this mess. But you always try to disobey, always want to run. Happy to live like a coward. Well, no more. I won't allow it. There will be no more running!' He was screaming now, and Danni could see a bulging vein on his forehead even from this distance.

'Please,' Danni pleaded, begging him, hoping he would realise what was really happening. 'You're scaring the children. And you've hit Leah. You've never hit our children before.'

'Because we were too lenient,' Jon said. 'And it clearly hasn't worked. So we need to change things. Instill a bit of discipline. No more namby-pamby, tip-toeing around things. I'm getting tired of saying this, so I'm going to give you all one last chance. Get back in the fucking house.'

'And if we don't?'

Jon laughed. It was an utterly humourless one. 'Then I'll drag each of you back in myself. It's your choice.'

Danni gave up, he was too far gone to be reasoned with. As scared, horrified, and sad as that made her, all that mattered right now was her children. And Danni knew that Jon, the real Jon, the one lost to them right now, would agree.

'Okay,' she said, finally. 'We'll go inside, Jon. Whatever you say.'

He squinted his eyes at her and cocked his head to the side like a confused dog. 'Is that so?'

'Yes,' she said and nodded. 'Kids, on your feet.'

'But, Mom,' Leah said, sobbing.

'Don't argue, Leah,' Danni said, raising her voice. 'Move. Now.'

Reluctantly, Leah stood back up. She moved next to her brother and let him bear his weight on her. Danni realised that his crutches were still upstairs in the bedroom above. She cursed herself for not tossing them out first before she had jumped. But, given the situation, forward planning hadn't been high on her list. Her body, wracked with pain, would testify to that.

'Good,' Jon said. 'I'm glad you're all seeing sense.'

Danni smiled as best she could and limped over to him. 'We'll try it your way, hun,' she said and dropped an arm around his shoulders, letting him take her weight as Leah had done for Alex. He complied, standing strong for her.

'Okay,' he said. 'Everything will be better this way, you'll see. We can be happy here.'

'Okay, Jon' Danni said. She let herself be led towards the door. 'We'll give it a try. I promise.'

'You won't regret it,' Jon said, his smile a crooked one. He pushed open the front door and turned to his family, gesturing for them to go inside. 'After you,' he said.

Danni smiled and nodded. She took a step onto her good leg and prepared for the pain she knew she would feel.

Then she acted.

She quickly swung her other foot up as hard as she physically could, aiming a vicious kick right into Jon's groin. Her ankle throbbed with fresh pain at the force of impact, but she knew it was worth it. Jon's eyes shot open, eyeballs nearly popping from his skull, and he let out a pained shriek. He dropped to his knees, shuddering, hands pressed between his legs. Danni reached down and grabbed one of the clay plant pots beside the door—one with a withered, dead plant within.

She swung it.

There was a dull thud, and while the pot did not break, the force of the strike vibrated up the length of Danni's arms. Jon's head snapped to the side and he fell, letting out a sharp groan.

Danni dropped the potted plant and dug through Jon's pockets as he flailed on the floor. He was trying to speak, but what came out was slurred and incomprehensible. She saw his eyes roll in his head, struggling to focus and adjust.

And she prayed she hadn't caused any real damage to him.

Danni quickly found what she was looking for and stood back up, keys to the SUV in hand. Her body still hurt, but she pushed past that.

'To the car,' she yelled, grabbing at her children and pushing them away from their father.

'But what about Dad?'

'I know, Alex,' she said, 'but we need to go. I'll come back for him, but right now it isn't safe.'

Thankfully, neither child put up any resistance. They were clearly frightened and confused, but could sense that something wasn't right. Both Leah and Danni, who was now badly limping, helped Alex as they ran as quickly as they could to the vehicle. Danni's head was still spinning from the fall, and her stomach lurched. She fought the feeling of nausea and unlocked the car with a click of the fob.

Leah and Alex piled into the back and Danni hopped

into the driver's side, slamming the door behind her. She started the engine.

'Seat belts,' she ordered, knowing that she was really going to floor it. She put the car in gear, about to set off, when a loud smack on the rear windscreen startled them all. Both Leah and Alex screamed, and in her rearview mirror Danni saw that Jon was standing behind the car, blood spilling from a cut on his forehead.

His eyes were wide and his nose flared as he screamed incoherently. Danni had never seen her husband look that way before.

It was almost psychopathic.

Danni flicked the switch to her side, automatically locking all the doors, and revved the engine. She pushed the pedal to the floor and set off, kicking up dirt behind them and showering Jon as she did. The car raced down the driveway to the main road ahead, and Danni could see Jon's silhouette running after them.

She swung the vehicle in a wide turn out onto the road, not braking, and praying she wouldn't turn out into any traffic. Thankfully, the road was clear.

Her ankle flared in pain again as she worked the clutch, and she whipped the wheel around, trying to right the vehicle onto the road. The children screamed as Danni pulled the other way now, trying to straighten up, but she overcompensated, and the car veered. Danni tried to correct it again, but pulled back too hard, and the car began swinging wildly from one side of the road to the other as she struggled to control it.

Danni finally thought she had it, when the wheel slipped from the tarmac into grass and hit something. A branch? A log? She wasn't sure, but the car bounced violently, causing another shriek from the children. The

SUV turned quickly on itself, swinging ninety degrees and going much too fast.

The momentum tilted the car, making it top heavy, and it began to roll onto its side. Danni felt her world spin.

Amongst the shrieks of terror from the children, she heard the strain of metal and the smashing of glass. The noises were deafening, and all Danni could think about was Leah and Alex. She was terrified she may have killed them.

The car was still rolling when Danni's head bounced off the window beside her, and she blacked out completely.

20

Danni was in her room back home.

She didn't like calling it that; home. Because it felt like a prison.

She was young, sixteen, just finished school. She'd received her exam results, and they had been okay, better than expected, but not ground-breaking.

It was a milestone in her life. And she should have been happy about that. But, in Danni's life, there wasn't much to be happy about.

Living with her father made her miserable and terrified in equal measure. And things were getting worse.

For as long as Danni could remember, her father had always been mean and cranky, and sometimes downright cruel. Amongst this misery were periodic, nightmarish spikes, such as chasing her out into the garden and beating her, locking her in the spare room, more beatings, even trapping her alone in the mill, but it seemed like everything was building towards something.

Something gut-wrenchingly vile.

'Danni,' her father bellowed from below.

She was on her bed, reading a magazine, and debated

ignoring him completely. But she knew that would only lead to bad things.

Please leave me alone, please leave me alone, please leave me alone.

'Danni,' he yelled, again. 'You get down here right now.'

His voice had that tone again. Something beyond anger. There was a hatred there, a loathing that she could detect when things were at their worst.

How could someone hate their own daughter like that? His own flesh and blood?

What had she done to deserve this?

'I'm reading, Dad,' she called back down. A mistake, she knew. Answering back only drove him further into a rage, especially when he was like this. But she couldn't help it, she was tired of feeling so alone and afraid.

So helpless.

'Don't you dare ignore me, girl,' he shouted back. She heard his heavy footsteps stomp through from the hall to the bottom of the stairs. 'So help me, if I have to come up there, you're gonna regret it. Do you understand me?'

She thought of her mother.

Danni could only remember her a little, her maternal face recognisable only from a photograph Danni had managed to keep from her father, who seemed intent on destroying them all. In this picture, her mother looked happy, so did Dad, and they had their arms around each other in a loving embrace. They were standing outside of a terraced house—their first home together.

But this picture seemed to clash with the emotions that stirred in Danni when she thought of her mother. Rather, memories of her were more impressions of sadness and misery.

'I'm coming,' Danni shouted back down. She took a breath and slowly climbed off the bed before walking out to the landing. She looked down at her father as he stood at the foot of the stairs.

Even from this elevated vantage point, he was an imposing figure; a big man with a big frame. And even though age had started to take its toll, he still seemed like a giant to Danni.

Maybe that was all in her head.

His jaw was clenched, and his nicotine-stained fingers wiggled with a pent-up energy. Eventually, they curled into fists.

'Come down,' he ordered.

She didn't want to. She wanted to turn and run, maybe climb from her window and take her chances with the drop. Then she could keep running, on and on and on. Her father was big, but he wasn't quick. She could run into infinity, and he would never catch her.

It was a comforting thought.

'Now!' he screamed, the volume causing Danni to jump.

Slowly, she made her way down towards him, each step tentative as the wooden stairs creaked under her weight. A nasty smile crept over his lips.

'What do you want?' she asked, stopping halfway down her descent.

His smile widened, and he ran his tongue over his bottom lip. 'Come down and see,' he said.

A feeling of deep dread bloomed in her stomach. This was going to be bad. Worse than anything that had come before.

She just knew it.

But enough was enough. She would suffer no more.

'No,' she told him.

His smile vanished, replaced in an instant by a hateful scowl. 'What did you say to me?'

'I said no. I want this to stop.'

'You little bitch,' he said. Flecks of spittle popped from his mouth.

'Dad, look at yourself. Think about what you're doing,' Danni pleaded. 'Why do you hate me so much? Why do you do these

things? I'm your daughter, you're supposed to love me. You're not supposed to...' but she couldn't finish. Instead, she broke down crying and looked at him with wet, pleading eyes.

Something in him changed.

His scowl fell away and his face softened, as if the remnants of a once-good man were again taking hold.

Then he shook his head.

His lip curled.

And his fists clenched again.

'You horrible little cunt.'

Whatever flash of clarity had come over him had clearly been buried once again. He stomped a heavy foot onto the first step.

'Dad, please.'

'Little bitch.'

His words were laced with venom, and he spat them through gritted teeth.

He took another step, and another. And for every step he took, Danni backed up one as well.

Her father then quickened, springing up two steps in a single bound. Instinctively, Danni spun and ran up the stairs herself.

Knowing the chase was on.

She bounded to the top as fast as she could, desperate to get away from him, and turned into the hallway before sprinting back to her room. The whole time, she could hear her father's booming footfalls as he chased her and felt his presence looming. She nipped through the door and slammed it shut, pressing her back up against it.

'Dad, please,' *she pleaded. The door had no lock, and she knew she couldn't hold him off. She heard him thunder down the hall towards her before he started banging and pushing against the door.*

'Open the fucking door, now,' *he yelled, striking his big fists* against the thick wood that separated them. The force of his blows caused the door to shake.

'Please calm down.'

The brass handle twisted and turned, and then she felt another thump against the wood. It happened again, and she knew he was lunging into it from the other side, causing her to jolt half a step forward. She quickly regained her footing and threw herself backward, pushing the door shut. She pressed herself into it as hard as she could.

He hit the door again with even more force, and Danni was flung forward. This time, however, she doubled over and lost her balance. She twisted, and fell to her rear, but acted quickly and scuttled back again, slamming her back into the door, trying to force it shut. She pushed with her legs, with everything she had, to keep it closed.

To keep him outside.

Maybe, if she could hold him off long enough, the rage would clear and he would leave her alone.

But the door smashed into her again, harder and harder, nudging her forward. The edge of the door painfully found her spine and dug in as her father forced it open. Danni cried helplessly as she slid forward.

Old Arthur made his entry.

Danni jumped to her feet and ran towards the window, determined to pull it open and throw herself out. Then, whatever would be would be. If she killed herself during the fall, well, right now she didn't really care.

But it was not to be. She felt his strong grip on the back of her neck and his meaty fingers closed round it, actually big enough that the tips pressed on her windpipe. It felt like if he squeezed, only a little, her head would actually pop.

He didn't squeeze, though.

Instead, he threw her sideways.

Danni's feet left the floor for a few moments, and she crashed into the frame of the bed. Pain flared in her hipbone as it struck the wooden frame.

She cried out.

He was on her again in an instant, before she had a chance to get to her feet again. Before she could escape. He grabbed her hair and pulled her to her feet, spinning her to face him.

'Please,' she said, but the smirk on his face told her all she needed to know.

There would be no mercy for her.

His other hand again found its way around her neck. Danni was lifted painfully from the floor and thrown onto the bed.

'Going to teach you a lesson,' he said and pulled at his belt. It came free, and he dropped it to the floor before unbuttoning his trousers.

'No, not this. Please, not this.'

She pleaded to him.

To God.

Neither listened.

God didn't seem to give a fuck.

There would be no divine intervention.

Danni wept.

She hated him more than ever that night.

And that night was a long one.

A vile one.

A sickening one.

It was the worst moment of her life.

Mom, why did you leave me and let this happen?

The next morning, she packed as much as she could and fled from the house during the early hours.

She vowed never to go back.

21

'WAKE UP.'

Danni heard the voice; frantic and feminine. It seemed to swim into her consciousness from some faraway place.

She felt something sting the skin of her cheek, over and over again.

'Please wake up. We need to go. We need to help him.'

Nothing made sense. Part of Danni was still running away from home, and the actions of her father were still fresh in her mind.

She could still feel him on her. Smell him on her.

Another part of her, however, was being pulled away from the memory, as if rising up to the surface of a river, leaving the dream in the crushing black depths below.

'Wake up!'

The voice was louder now, screaming, and the force that slapped her cheek hit again, harder.

Hard enough to draw her back into consciousness.

Her eyes opened, and she instinctively drew in a sharp breath.

The first thing she noticed was the smell, a pungent tang of petrol.

Her head felt full, but weightless.

She opened her eyes and saw that everything was upside down.

The windscreen before her had shattered, leaving only jagged glass around the edges.

Another blow brought her to total awareness.

Leah was beside her, lying on what used to be the ceiling of the SUV, desperately trying to wake her. Danni looked over her body, trying to detect any injuries. Everything hurt, but she could pinpoint no extreme sources of discomfort. That meant that either she had been lucky in the crash, or she was running on adrenaline and something serious was just waiting to reveal itself.

She turned her head to her side, thankful that her neck moved with no trouble, and made eye contact with her daughter.

Leah looked terrified, and she had numerous scrapes on her face. Danni looked farther back, to the rear of the car.

Looking for her son.

'Alex?' she asked. Her voice was little more than a croak.

'He took him, Mom,' Leah said.

'What?'

'Dad,' she said. 'After we crashed. You wouldn't wake up, so I tried to get Alex out of the car on my own. Dad came racing down the road towards us. I ran, but he grabbed Alex and yanked him free. He said that if we wanted to see him again, we had to go back to the house. I screamed for Dad to stop, but he wouldn't listen.'

Leah was in hysterics, throwing the story out in breathless sentences.

Danni felt a renewed sense of panic and urgency swell up inside her, blowing away the last of the disoriented cobwebs. She moved a hand to her seatbelt, feeling it dig into her shoulder as the weight of her body pushed down onto it. She used her other hand to brace herself against the roof of the car, released the belt, and fell to the roof below. Leah moved aside and crawled backwards through the broken passenger-side window. Danni angled her body and squeezed herself through the same gap. She felt sharp glass press against her, cutting her as she crawled, but tried to ignore the stinging pain.

Her body was aching, and her ankle still throbbed intensely.

Once outside, she used the car to pull herself to her feet. Standing upright wasn't easy, but it was possible.

Danni could hear the trickle of liquid, and she started to limp forward away from the vehicle as Leah trotted ahead. 'Was Alex okay?' Danni asked.

'He hurt his arm in the crash,' Leah said. 'I don't know if it was broken, but he was screaming. When Dad dragged Alex out of the car, he didn't seem to care that Alex was hurt.'

Danni turned around to look at the state of the car that lay on its roof. The prognosis wasn't good.

Most of the windows were out, the metal was crumpled and twisted, and its paint was streaked along the road in random patterns. She saw a pool of liquid seeping out from one side of the vehicle—presumably petrol or oil—like a pool of blood.

If she did manage to get Alex out, they now had no way of escaping other than on foot.

She cursed herself.

So eager had she been to get her children away to safety that she had been careless.

Maybe Jon had been right. Her desire to run, to always flee from difficult situations, had now cost her. The car was fucked, Alex had been taken, and she and her daughter were alone and unprepared for what they had to do next.

'Mom,' Leah said, 'we need to go. Alex is back there. We need to help him.'

'Okay,' Danni answered, trying desperately to form some kind of plan. She checked her pockets for her phone, but quickly realised she had left it inside. 'Do you have your phone?' Danni asked Leah.

Leah shook her head. 'It's back at the house.'

Damn it.

Calling the police for help was clearly a no-go. She could wait and hope someone drove past who could offer help. But the road was a quiet one, and Danni had no idea how long that would take.

That left only one option; she had to go back.

'You wait here,' Danni said to her daughter, intending to do this alone.

'What?'

'Keep away from the car and keep off the road as well. Stand in the field. Whoever comes by will have to stop—its hard to miss a car lying on its roof in the middle of the road. So when they do, you need to get them to call the police. Tell them where we are, and that we need help. I'll go and get Alex.'

'No,' Leah said.

'Don't argue, Leah. This isn't up for debate.'

'You're right, it isn't,' the girl said. 'And I'm not staying. Alex is in trouble, and I'm going to help. I'm not staying here while you run off and get yourself killed.'

'Leah—'

'No, Mom. I don't care what you say, I'm coming. You can't keep me here, anyway. Besides, you're hurt, and can hardly walk. It's going to take both of us.'

Danni looked her daughter up and down. The girl was scared and physically shaken. She had been through so much this weekend. Ever since the scare yesterday she had been a shell of her normal self, retreating inside to get away from what she couldn't understand.

It appeared now, however, that she'd had enough of being helpless. Now, her little girl was standing up for herself. And for her family.

Even in a situation such as this, a terrible and nightmarish one, Danni couldn't help but feel a swell of immense pride towards her daughter.

But she couldn't take her back to that house. Not when she knew, or partly knew, what was waiting for them inside. It was irresponsible to an extreme degree. What kind of parent would she be if she allowed that?

She shook her head, ready to have the final say, but Leah simply turned and started walking back to the house.

'Leah,' Danni shouted.

'Let's go, Mom,' her daughter said without looking back.

Danni limped after her, and as she did she became aware that Leah was actually right; Danni couldn't move very well. Her ankle still hurt terribly, and if that was the case, what good would she be to Alex?

'Wait, Leah,' Danni said.

'I already told you, Mom, I'm going.'

'I know,' Danni replied. At this, her daughter stopped and turned to face her. 'But I could do with a hand.'

Leah let slip a small smile and jogged back to her mother. Danni put an arm over her daughter's shoulders and let her take some of her weight. The two of them then made their way back to the house, slowly but steadily.

'Mom, what happened to Dad?' Leah asked. 'Why is he acting like this?'

'I don't know,' Danni said, though that wasn't strictly true. She'd read the diary, the one that was back at the house, and had a good idea of what was going on—as outlandish as it seemed. However, she didn't see the need to scare her daughter further with stories of evil things living in the mill. Though maybe it was past that point now.

'But he isn't himself, is he?' Leah asked.

'Not at the minute, sweetie, no.'

'Will he hurt Alex?'

'I don't know, Leah. I really don't. But he won't if I can help it.'

'And if we get Alex back? He'll try and hurt us as well, won't he?'

Danni paused, then nodded. It was pointless lying, because they needed to be prepared for the worst. 'Probably, yes.'

'This is so fucked up.'

Danni didn't even make a move to admonish her daughter for swearing. The girl had summed up the situation perfectly.

'Yes. It is.'

'So, those things we saw in there. They're real, aren't they?'

'Yeah,' Danni said. It sounded crazy to admit that, but there was no other answer.

Danni felt a chill run up her spine. It was ludicrous, absolutely bat-shit insane to think there were honest-to-god ghosts, or demons, or whatever the hell they were, back at the house. Impossible things that seemed only to want to cause pain.

And her own father was among them.

She remembered his black eyes, his cold touch, and shuddered again.

'I saw something last night too,' Leah said. 'An old woman in our room. The same one we saw before we ran. Do you think they are ghosts? People who used to live in the house?'

Danni was shocked her daughter had experienced another scare that she hadn't shared. She also considered her daughter's question, and didn't have an answer, but she did remember stories from when she was younger about an old woman. There was even a rhyme about her.

Old Mrs. Hobbes, all alone she sobs,
Dead and forgotten, underground and rotten,
Lying in her coffin, with her eyes wide open.

She wondered if this Mrs. Hobbes was the same old woman they had been seeing. It seemed to make sense, as insane as that sounded.

But none of this should have made any sense.

'I don't know,' Danni said, answering her daughter. 'But why didn't you say anything about that before? I had no idea.'

'Because I was scared,' Leah said. 'Scared of what happened, and scared of what you would all think of me.'

'You know you can tell me anything.'

'Yeah, I know, but I didn't know how Dad would take it. So, it seemed easier to keep it to myself and just try to get through it.'

Danni tightened her arm around Leah and gave her a hug.

'I'm sorry,' Danni said. 'We should never have come up here. It's my fault.'

'No,' Leah said, 'it's not.'

'You don't have to go through with this, you know,' Danni said, giving it one last throw of the dice. 'There's no shame in waiting here for me.'

'Yes, there is,' Leah said. 'Alex needs our help, and I'm not going to let him down. I'm not going to run.'

That struck a chord with Danni. She admired her daughter and wished she had been as brave when she was of a similar age.

They reached the turnoff for the road up to the house and paused. Danni could see the skid marks the SUV had left during her unsuccessful attempt at fleeing. She felt another pang of guilt for nearly killing her children with her recklessness and contemplated apologising to Leah for that, but didn't think her daughter would feel the need to accept it.

She looked back down the main road and saw their car on its roof—absolutely ruined—and could still smell the burnt, metallic aroma in the air. She then looked past the wrecked vehicle, hoping to see headlights approaching through the dark.

There was nothing.

They were on their own.

And it was time to go.

It was dark, but up in the distance she could make out the silhouette of the house, standing against the dark sky, and behind that, the tower-like mill. Both looked ominous, as if they were daring her to approach.

She hesitated, trying to find another option. Surely it was suicide to just walk into the jaws of death like this?

But one of her children was up there, and he desperately needed her. He needed them both.

Danni took a breath and gave her daughter another squeeze.

'I'm proud of you,' she said. 'And I love you.'

'Thanks, Mom. I love you too.'

With that, the two women made their way up the driveway.

22

HE STOOD, looking from the window.

Waiting for them to arrive.

As he knew they would.

The trap was set.

As if on cue, he saw two forms making their way towards the house. The taller one, who seemed to be struggling, leaned on the shorter. He recognised the older one as Dannielle, his daughter.

The other was a granddaughter he had never met.

And with good reason.

Why would she ever bring her family back here and introduce them to him? He had been a monster.

And not by choice.

The old evil that lived here on this land had gotten inside of him and twisted him into something he wasn't.

And the worst thing was, he couldn't stop it. The harder he fought, the more it took hold. Only when it was too late, and the thing had full control, did he realise what his dear wife, Alice, had gone through.

However, Alice had found a way to free herself before it was too late.

He hadn't been that smart.

Or that strong.

And so its hold became absolute, claiming him completely. It got inside, infesting him, taking his body and soul as its own.

But, if life had been bad under the control of that thing, in death it was worse.

So much worse.

It was beyond madness, beyond pain, beyond torture. He had no real form to ever inhabit again, just a twisted echo of it. And Arthur was simply a bystander, a puppet on a string manipulated to follow his master's whims and desires. An endless torment, existing with no agency of his own.

He was nothing more than a floating consciousness that was used and played with as desired.

And there was more.

Bad enough he had to watch what was happening to his daughter and her family while they were in this house, and watch as the thing that owned him started to seep into the husband's consciousness as well, but there was the never ending-pain he felt.

That same agony that had been present ever since he had died and re-awoken like this.

And pain was different in this existence. It was at once constant, and yet ever-changing and undulating. It wasn't quite physical—he wasn't a physical thing anymore—but he suffered it none the less. It felt as if he were rotting away, that his consciousness was souring and being torn apart, again and again.

This was a torture that would never let up. Never end.

It was eternal.

He was trapped between two places: here in his home, a prison in life and in death, but also somewhere else.

Somewhere worse

He knew it was the place this hideous thing had originated from.

A nightmarish place that touched the edges of his own world, but was removed from it. A place of chaos, desecration, and malevolence.

Through whatever connection the monster had over him in its control of him, he would see this place sometimes —exist there for a while, until needed.

And he learned a very surprising thing: he knew that this demonic entity—if that term was actually accurate, which he suspected it was not—that now owned his soul, was actually scared in this place. Through his connection to it, he could somehow sense its fear, and came to learn it was a lower being that managed to find a refuge in his world. A place for it to hide. There were other things in this place, many unimaginable things, beings he could scarcely comprehend that terrified him beyond understanding.

That ripped at his mind and sanity.

But, the old entity that resided on this land, that had taken residence here long ago, was the danger his daughter would face. And it was a danger that would claim her very soul for eternity if she could not overcome it.

And worse, he would be part of it.

He would only be able to watch as the vile creature from that terrifying other place used his own twisted image to terrorise and torture what he prized, and loved, more than anything else in this world. He would feel her as it made him do things, as it did when he was alive; things that tortured his mind.

And he also knew, however, of the one thing that would weaken this demon's hold on their world. An element that could scorch the link and give his daughter and her family a chance to escape.

He prayed Dannielle was strong enough to overcome this.

He wanted that more than anything.

But, he just couldn't see how it was possible.

23

AFTER REACHING THE HOUSE, Danni considered where to look first. The mill seemed an obvious place to start; it was small and wouldn't take long to search. Also, the thing behind all this, whatever it was, seemed to have an affinity with that place.

However, she heard something that diverted her attention and removed the need to make any choice at all.

A noise from inside the house. Faint, but definitely there.

Click, click, click.

'That's Alex,' Danni said.

Danni turned towards the house and jogged to the front door, trying to bear as much weight on her ankle as she could. Leah kept pace, helping Danni move, but was confused.

'What do you mean?' she asked. 'I didn't hear anything.'

'His crutches,' Danni said. 'I heard him moving.'

They stopped just before the entrance and Danni listened, trying to hear signs of her son again.

But there was nothing.

'What should we do?' Leah asked.

Danni put her hand on the handle and pushed the door open. 'We go in.'

The hallway inside was dark and cold. Danni stepped over the threshold and tried the light switch. The lights flicked on, then immediately blew, popping the bulbs with a bang. Leah let out a brief shriek and hugged her mother tight. Danni wasn't sure if she had caught a glimpse—just before the lights blew—of a figure standing at the top of the stairs.

If she had, could it have been Alex? Or something else...

Danni pressed on, because she knew that she would likely have to go through hell here in order to find her son. She decided to check the ground floor first, though she didn't hold out much hope, knowing things wouldn't be that easy.

She was a fly, knowingly entering the spider's web.

Ready to be caught and devoured.

The living room gave up nothing and there was no one inside, so they moved into the kitchen. Leah clutched onto Danni's arm, and Danni felt her daughter trembling. Regardless, the girl still moved forward. She was fighting through her fear.

They both were.

The kitchen was also deserted, as was the dining room, both cast in darkness like the rest of the house. Danni was about to turn back when she saw movement through the glazed double-doors of the dining room that looked out to the back of the house.

It had been a fleeting movement, but Danni was certain.

She started to walk over to the doors, needing to check just to see if it was Alex. Maybe he'd gotten free and escaped outside? When she reached her destination, she looked out through the glazing to the rear garden. She couldn't see much through the night, but whatever she had seen move before wasn't there now. She contemplated shouting, to see if she could draw it back.

But she had no need to.

Something moved, revealing itself from the darkness outside.

Leah screamed and backpeddled.

The old woman, Margaret Hobbes, stood directly outside of the glass doors.

Close up, Danni could now see all the horrible details of the grinning old woman's face.

Her pale, ashen skin was actually lined with thin, dark veins. The pupils of her eyes had a tinge of striking yellow to them, and they glinted in the darkness. Her thin hands were linked before her midsection, and the long, plain dress she wore, one with a high collar surrounding her neck, actually had a subtle, embossed pattern to it. Her grey hair was up in a bun, and her smile was wide enough to show blackened gums and teeth.

Danni's body initially locked up in fear upon seeing this wretched woman. In short order, however, anger emboldened her. She gritted her teeth, walked up to the glass and slammed the flat of her palms against it.

'What the fuck do you want from us?' Danni screamed.

The woman continued to grin, but stayed motionless.

'We need to run,' Leah said from behind, pressing herself against the wall.

'Where is my son?' Danni demanded and slapped her palm on the glass again. 'Tell me, you fucking bitch!'

Still the woman remained motionless, the only hint of understanding, or emotion, her continued, cruel, mocking smile.

Click, click, click.

Danni snapped her head around, again hearing her son. It sounded like he was close, literally right beside her, but when she turned, there was no one there. Danni felt a sudden burst of cold, and a horrible, rotting smell assaulted her.

She turned her head back, but didn't have time to scream.

The old woman was now on the inside of the glass door, standing directly in front of Danni, practically nose to nose.

The old witch's smile changed into a wide-eyed scowl, and she grabbed Danni around the throat with hands so cold that their touch felt like a burn. The grip was powerful, and Danni felt herself pushed back, her feet lifted from the floor as the woman moved through the air.

Danni's back slammed into the wall, and in her peripheral vision she saw Leah slide out of their way. The old woman then lifted Danni up higher, leaving her legs dangling and kicking in the air. The hands closed tighter, cutting off the last trickle of oxygen Danni was able to suck into her lungs.

'We... *want*,' the old woman started to say, her words slow and laboured, a strain to get out. Her lips did not move. '*Your... family.*'

Danni kicked her legs out, trying to catch the woman in the gut. Trying to fight free. However, her feet just glided through the space where the woman's body should have been. Danni then brought her hands up to try to pull the old hag's hands away, to stop the strangulation, but found only her own throat to touch.

As if the old woman wasn't even there.

And yet, Danni was suspended in the air, and the life was being choked from her. She could see the vile woman before her, but could not physically touch her. That twisted grin returned.

Danni felt something else, too. Another, smaller set of hands grabbed her wrist. She looked down and saw Leah standing beside her. The poor girl looked absolutely terrified, but she began to pull at Danni.

'Let her go,' the girl yelled and pulled again. 'Let my mom go!'

Danni saw blotches of light spring up in her vision as she desperately tried to gulp in some air. Her head hurt terribly, and she started to feel dizzy and light-headed. She felt Leah move, stepping in closer, and then her daughter grabbed Danni tight around the waist. There shouldn't have been room between Danni and the old woman, but Leah and the hag seemed to be occupying the same space somehow. Leah again heaved and let out a primal scream.

Then, Danni felt her body fall to the side, suddenly breaking free of the iron-like grip. She dropped to the floor in a tangled mess with her daughter and quickly began to suck in deep, desperate breaths. As Danni tried to orientate herself, she looked up to where the old woman had been only moments ago.

She was there no longer.

They both heard a menacing cackle that slowly faded out to nothing.

Leah wrapped her hands around Danni and hugged her tightly. The girl began to sob, loudly.

'I'm so proud of you,' Danni said, once she had enough air back into her lungs to do so. Her vision had come into focus again, but her head still throbbed, and her throat felt raw.

'I was so scared,' Leah said, burying her face into Danni's chest.

'I know you were, sweetie,' Danni answered, getting to her feet. They stood together, and Danni cupped Leah's cheek, looking directly into her daughter's wet eyes. 'I know you were scared. But you saved me, hun, scared or not.'

'I don't know if I can do this.'

'Yes, you can,' Danni said. 'Look at what you just did. You saved me. I know it's terrifying, and I know it feels easier to just turn and run away, but what you did took courage. You stood up to what was scaring you. That gives you power. You saved me, so what say we go and save your brother, too?'

Leah took a moment. She still sobbed, and still clung to Danni, but Danni could see a slow change come over the girl. The crying eased, and her breathing deepened. Leah closed her eyes and took a few more breaths.

Then, she opened her eyes again. The fear was still there, but so, too, was a measure of resolve.

'Okay,' she said. 'Let's go get Alex. And Dad.'

Danni nodded, again proud of her girl.

But Danni had her doubts. Leah obviously wanted to help her father, but Danni just couldn't see how they could. Saving Alex would be hard enough, but she had no idea if she could pull Jon back to sanity. And, the fact that her focus was solely on their son meant she was, consciously or subconsciously, ready to leave her husband behind.

24

LEAH'S MOTHER led her up the stairs, taking slow and steady steps. The treads creaked beneath them as they ascended.

Leah's heart was pumping so fast it felt like it was going to beat its way through her chest cavity. She had never experienced prolonged fear like this and was on the cusp of losing the slim grip she had on her sanity.

But her mother had been right.

After she had seen that old woman throw Danni against the wall, Leah was sure her mother was going to die. Right in front of her eyes. And then that demon would turn its attentions to her.

She had seen the desperation on her mother's face while fear had frozen Leah to the spot. The thought of her mom—the woman who had birthed and raised her—dying scared her more than anything else she had experienced this weekend. And it also brought with it a surge of anger. In an instant, Leah had grabbed hold of that anger and used it, refusing to just lie down and let things happen to her, or her mother.

She had acted.

And, it turned out, saved her mother's life.

She was still scared, terrified, but her mother was right; she had stood up to the thing that scared her, and she had stared it down. That didn't make it any less scary, but it gave her the confidence to go on. To keep trying.

And now, Alex needed her.

She had always been there for him before and never let him down in her life. She would not start now. They reached the top of the stairs and paused on the landing. Leah peered into the darkness of the corridor, trying to make out whatever might be lurking in the shadows.

'Alex?' her mother called out, making Leah jump. It seemed any notion of stealth had now been totally discarded.

There was no reply.

So they moved down the corridor, farther into the dark while checking each room as they went. They peeked into the bathroom, and Leah shuddered as she remembered the previous night—showering as that horrible man watched her.

Thankfully, the bathroom was empty. As was the first spare room. Then they came to the master bedroom, the one that belonged to Leah's grandfather. A man she had never known.

'Alex,' Danni called again, and Leah managed not to jump this time. Yet again, there was no reply.

Leah found that curious.

Only a little while earlier as they stood outside, her mother swore she heard Alex's crutches as he moved through the house somewhere. So, if he could no longer yell for help, did that mean something had happened to him?

Her thoughts ran to the incident downstairs as well. One moment, the old woman had been standing outside then, after they were both distracted, she appeared inside, and attacked. Although, it wasn't the attack that concerned her at the moment, it was the distraction.

The trickery.

Suddenly, they heard it again—*click, click, click*. It sounded close. Close enough to be in the room before them.

Danni pushed the bedroom door open and stepped inside.

It felt wrong to Leah.

'No,' she whispered.

'What is it?' Danni asked

'It's a trick,' she said. 'This whole thing is a trap.' The door then suddenly slammed shut between them, confirming her fears.

Leah heard her mother bang on the other side, and Leah followed suit. She pushed at the door, but it was stuck fast, not yielding even a fraction.

'Leah,' she heard her mother call from inside the bedroom. 'Are you okay?'

'I think so,' Leah said, feeling a growing sense of panic. Being beside her mother gave her extra strength, extra conviction and courage, but now... now she was alone.

Her mother's banging stopped.

'Mom?' Leah yelled and kicked at the door. Then, she heard something that made her body lock up.

Breathing.

Slow, laboured breathing.

She turned her head and looked back down the dark corridor to the landing at the top of the stairs.

She saw him there.

His head was high enough to almost touch the ceiling. His jaw hung loose; the skin torn and ravaged.

It was the same man, the same *thing*, from the previous

night. The one who had watched her in the shower with that wild, predatory expression. His breathing quickened, as if growing excited.

'Mom?' Leah managed to squeak out. 'I need help.'

DANNI HEARD her daughter's words, but she could do nothing to help. The door would not budge.

And, only moments after it had slammed shut, she heard something.

Click, click, click.

Even before she turned to look, Danni knew deep down that it wasn't Alex. He had never been in the house—she had been tricked and lured here.

But something else was in the room with her.

She heard a voice. '*Dannielle.*'

It was little more than a whisper, but dripped with vile intent. Danni already knew who it belonged to. She turned to see her father standing in the middle of the room.

She was gripped by fear and unable to move. Outside, she could hear Leah screaming and kicking at the door again, frantic.

Danni pulled her hands up behind her back and grabbed the door handle, yanking at it again, but to no avail. Whatever force was holding it closed was not going to release it.

Her father laughed and slowly began to move towards her. He didn't walk, just moved forward, with that taunting, diabolical smile etched in place.

Danni's breath locked in her throat, and she tightened up. At the same time, she heard her daughter scream.

'No, stay away from me!'

Her father stopped, inches from her face. She could feel that intense cold again, and smell that disgusting stench.

The stench of the dead.

'*My... sweet... Danielle. Come... to... dear... old... dad.*'

'Leave me alone,' Danni whispered.

He started to laugh.

THIS WAS THE TORTURE, the true evil, that the ancient thing was capable of.

The pain of seeing his wife slip away from him and take her own life had been terrible. Losing himself to it was worse. What he did to Danni that terrible night tore him up inside, in ways that were unimaginable. The ultimate horror, and the ultimate shame, in one vile experience.

But, he knew now the true, malevolent power that the thing had. Simply turning people mad and taking their lives was not enough.

Lives were finite.

This was eternal.

It would own and control whatever was left of Arthur for the rest of time. And it would force him, again and again, to live out vile acts against innocent people.

But this?

This was to be the worst of it. He knew that the thing had no intention of letting Danielle and her family die just yet.

It would hurt them, break them, and totally destroy them. And, after it eventually took their lives, and made him kill his own daughter, their nightmare would begin anew. More terrible than ever before, and it would be everlasting.

Then they would be forced to experience taking an innocent life.

'Give me back my son,' he heard his daughter say. 'Where is he?'

Arthur's hand rose up—he had no choice in the matter —and caressed her cheek. A voice came from the space he inhabited, but it was not his own.

He had no voice any longer.

'With... his... father. And... our... master. Where... it... likes... to... dwell.'

Laughter now. Again, not from Arthur, but from the form he was a part of.

He prayed.

Arthur had never been a religious man in life, and now that he had seen a small glimpse of other, nightmarish places in death, he knew there was no God. There couldn't be. But he prayed, regardless, to something, anything that might be listening.

Let my daughter find the strength to save herself.

Then he turned his desperation to Danielle, willing his thoughts to be heard by her. He spoke again, the vile message of the demon coming through him.

'We... will... be... together... forever.'

He swept up a pale thumb and ran it over her lower lip. Danielle was shaking. She closed her eyes, and tears spilled down her face. He was causing this fear, and pain, and anguish, and he would continue to do so until she was too weak to fight back any longer.

Then it would own her.

Please, find a way to fight this. You are stronger than we were, Danielle. Find something to fuel your fight.

They both heard screams erupt from the hallway. Terrible, horrified screams from the young girl.

Danielle opened her eyes.

'No more,' she said, in an oddly restrained voice. Though unnervingly calm, a storm of emotion seemed to bubble below the surface. 'I'm tired of being scared of you. Of this place. Fuck you. You won't beat me. You hear? Fuck you!'

She was now screaming.

She then flung herself forward with a roar, and Arthur felt her actually pass through his form. He whipped round, or rather he was turned, and saw that Danielle was equally surprised, but was no longer pinned into a corner. As the young girl's cries continued from outside, Danielle's surprise was quickly replaced by a look of determination. She clenched her fists together.

Then she acted.

She reached her hand out, grabbed one of the bottles of scotch that stood on the nightstand, and hurled it towards him. It broke against the door. Arthur felt himself smiling and laughing. Danielle grabbed a fuller bottle next and hurled that too, desperate in her attempts to fend him off. That bottle hit the jamb of the door and erupted, spilling alcohol directly below him.

It was all useless, he knew that, but at least Danielle was fighting. Then, she grabbed whatever else she could: clothes, an old book, more bottles of alcohol, an entire drawer, and hurled those, cursing as she did so.

'Fuck you,' she screamed, and threw more that she could find. 'Fuck you. Fuck you. Fuck you.'

Danielle kept going, then grabbed the bedside lamp. Even though it was still connected to the electrical socket, she threw it as well, the cord long enough to let the lamp glide through the air and meet its target. Like everything else, it, too, passed through Arthur and struck the wall behind, smashing the glass shade and dropping to the floor. It bounced off the now wet timber floorboards, and the bulb smashed as well.

Arthur noticed a small blue flash from the prongs of the lamp beneath the smashed bulb, and small sparks spat to the floor.

A floor that was now soaked with alcohol.

Danielle was still throwing whatever she could and swearing her mantra of *fuck you*, over and over again while she was doing it, and it took a while for her to realise what was happening. The alcohol, and the clothes and other rubbish, caught light. The flames were small at first, but quickly began to spread, fuelled by the alcohol.

It may have just been luck, but this gave Arthur hope. She had stumbled upon the one thing he knew could help her.

Fire.

Arthur's connection to that thing made him privy to some of its knowledge, fears, and memories. He didn't understand how it worked, but he knew that fire, somehow, was able to affect the demon's hold. Just as it had years ago, when the townspeople of Bishops Hill had burned the farm to the ground. They had, completely by accident, stripped the vile monster of some of its power and control, and it had taken time for that power to rebuild.

However, help though it could, he knew that fire would never really hurt the demon, or kill it, since you can't kill the unkillable. But, perhaps, it could be used to give Danielle time.

Give her a chance.

The room glowed as the fire took hold, burning through the clothes and other items piled on the floor. It even began to crawl up the wall, following the trail of scotch, running up to the impact point of one of the bottles.

Arthur watched the flames. Somewhere far away he suddenly felt the demon's anger and despair. As the fire grew, it started to cloud things for the monster, Arthur could sense. He then felt his consciousness start to blur and knew he was being removed from this room, probably to be sent back to that hellish place.

It both terrified him and thrilled him. Perhaps Danielle could survive, if only for a little longer.

Arthur lifted up his head to look again at his daughter, for what might be the last-ever time. He was filled with a profound sadness at the misery he'd caused her in life. Whether intentional or not, he'd still played a part in it. He hadn't been strong enough for her. But, he was also proud to see her showing the fight and resolve that he had lacked.

Things became even more unclear, and he was almost too late in realising something; when he had lifted his head to look at his daughter, he had done so of his own volition. It hadn't just happened to him, it wasn't the actions of a puppet master, he had done it himself. Arthur realised that if the fire had severed the link, it had somehow given him some control.

If only for a brief time.

'Danielle,' he called, once more feeling his own voice, however disembodied it was. 'Use the fire. Use the fire to—'

But that was all he managed to get out before he was gone and sent back to that hell.

25

DANNI WASN'T sure what the hell had just happened, but she did know that she now had an opportunity to get out.

The fire that she'd inadvertently started was taking over the door, almost covering it completely, so she ran over, fighting through the flames, and grabbed the metal door handle.

It was hot and burned her hand. She cried out in pain, but didn't let go. Instead, she pulled at it and the door, thankfully, swung open. Danni then rushed out into the hallway and saw Leah rising to her feet.

The girl looked horrified and was wheezing. Her eyes were bloodshot.

'What happened?' Danni asked, grabbing hold of her daughter.

'That man,' she said through strained breaths. 'He was here, and he attacked me. He started to choke me, and then... I... I don't know. He was just gone.'

Danni didn't have time to try to figure out what had happened. They still needed get Alex, and now the bedroom behind them was spreading its fire. She grabbed her daughter's hand and pulled her along the hallway, heading quickly down the stairs.

'We need to go,' Danni told her.

'What about Alex?'

'He isn't here,' Danni said, remembering what her father had told her.

With his father, and our master. Where it likes to dwell.

She realised that she should have just followed her initial instinct all along and headed straight to the mill. But they had been drawn, tricked, into the house.

'How do you know?' Leah asked.

'Because I do. And I know where he is.'

But, before they ran from the house, Danni needed to grab something else. They reached the bottom of the stairs and quickly doubled back, heading to the kitchen. Leah kept pace, even though she was clearly confused.

Danni ran straight to the kitchen cupboards and began to rifle through them, hoping that her father had kept a more extensive stash of alcohol than was in his bedroom.

The last cupboard she opened revealed what she was looking for.

There had to be close to ten bottles of spirits in it, most looking like scotch, but some were clear.

She grabbed them, handing some to Leah.

'What are you doing?' Leah asked.

'Start pouring them out, everywhere you can.'

Danni started to do just that and clicked on the gas stove.

'I don't get it,' Leah said, but she emptied out one of the clear bottles, regardless, onto the kitchen work-surface. It smelled like vodka.

'We're burning this place down,' Danni said. She could smell the smoke drift down from upstairs; the fire was obviously spreading. Danni grabbed an old takeout menu from one of the drawers, held it to the gas stove, and it quickly took flame.

She carefully held it to a pool of the liquid on the floor and that too went up. She grabbed another couple of bottles and the mop from the corner of the kitchen.

'Why are we burning everything?' Leah asked.

It was a fair question, but not one there was time to answer. How could she explain to Leah that the ghost of her father, who had only moments before tried to attack her, seemed to momentarily regain some of his humanity and told her how to fight these things?

Use the fire.

It could well have been another trick, the same kind of misdirection that had lured them into the house in the first place, but she didn't think it was. She had seen a change in… whatever the hell he was. Her father? An entity? Regardless, she had seen the malevolence dissipate, revealing something beneath.

Maybe that was her real father, the one she had barely known.

And, he had given her something: knowledge that could help. Hell, she had seen it work. The fire she'd started must have been the reason he vanished, because up until that point he had been focused only on tormenting and hurting her.

She didn't need to know how, or why, it worked, only that it did.

Danni quickly stripped off her over-shirt, revealing only a white tank top beneath.

'Mom, what are you doing?' Leah asked.

'Getting us a weapon,' Danni answered.

She handed the bottles she was carrying over to Leah

and put a foot on the damp head of the mop. She yanked hard at the handle and in a single motion pulled it free. She then wrapped her shirt around one end of the wooden staff as tightly as she could, making sure it was secure in place. Then she doused it in alcohol before holding it over a nearby flame.

The head of her improvised torch ignited.

The fire in the kitchen was now really starting to spread, and the smoke worked its way into her throat, causing Danni to cough.

'Come on,' she said.

Before they could move, thunderous banging sounds erupted around them, startling them almost to the point that Danni dropped her torch. The impossibly loud sounds continued again and again, almost in anger.

In protest.

Cupboard doors flung open and then slammed closed over and over, and the heavy dining room table splintered, then broke apart, shards of its wood spraying everywhere.

Something was obviously pissed.

'Mom,' Leah yelled. 'What's happening?'

Danni pulled her through to the hallway to escape, but it seemed things would not be that easy.

The old hag and the tall man with the dislocated jaw both stood in front of the door, both motionless.

Danni didn't even stop to think. She took one of the bottles from Leah and hurled it to the floor at the feet of the things that barred their exit.

Then another.

She tried to hold the torch out in front, as if it would ward off the entities like a crucifix to a vampire, but the old woman was on her quickly. The hag moved towards Danni with frightening speed and grabbed her by the throat, slamming her against the side of the stairs. The tall man advanced as well.

Danni struggled with the thing, but, as before, it was like fighting smoke. She quickly extended the arm with the torch to Leah, who was screaming in terror.

'Fire,' Danni croaked as the man took hold of her as well. She felt his massive, cold hands grab her head and begin to squeeze. The pain was immense, and she felt like her skull could crack at any moment.

Danni felt the torch leave her grip, but her eyes were now shut tight, an instinctive reaction to the pain.

Still she fought; kicking and lashing out, but all of it was useless.

'Hey!' she heard Leah shout. Then she heard another bottle break. Danni thought her skull was about to cave in completely.

Then she felt heat.

And the pressure eased up. The hold on her released.

Danni slid to the floor and managed to open her eyes. Her vision was blurred, but she could make out her daughter, standing close to flames that now blocked the exit— flames that were quickly engulfing everything around them. The two entities stood, looking at Leah, their forms beginning to fade away.

'Come on, Mom,' Leah yelled desperately. Danni began to crawl towards her daughter. The entities made no effort to stop them. Leah stepped forward and helped Danni to her feet.

They braced themselves and dashed forward through searing flames that licked at them and out into the cold night.

Danni dropped to her knees and began to cough and wheeze, purging the thick smoke from her body. Her head still throbbed with pain, and her vision was blurred. Slowly, she got to her feet and looked back inside to see the old woman and tall man completely melt away to nothing.

However, just before they vanished, Danni noticed that they looked... different.

More human, and their faces hung with a look of sorrow and regret.

Danni turned back to her daughter and saw that her skin was streaked and dirtied. Leah, too, was coughing, and Danni only now realised what kind of danger they had been in with so much fire and smoke billowing around them.

It had registered at the time, of course, but she was running on instinct, not knowing just how close they had come to being burned alive.

Leah, still holding the torch and one remaining bottle, hugged Danni and sobbed. Danni hated that she'd put her daughter through this, and hugged her back.

As scared, hurt, and exhausted as they both were, it was time to finish this.

'Are you ready?' she asked Leah, pulling away to look her daughter in the eyes. 'You can go back if you want. There's no shame in it.'

Leah raised her head, and Danni saw a look of grim determination.

'I'm ready,' she said, and the girl certainly looked it.

Danni nodded and took the torch from her. 'Okay,' she said, 'let's go save our family.'

Both women jogged quickly up towards the imposing mill ahead, barreling headlong into whatever was waiting.

26

THIS WAS IT. Danni could feel it.

It was time for them to end things.

Danni and Leah stood before the wooden door to the mill, which looked substantial, heavy, and more than a little weathered. Danni slapped a flat hand hard against the door.

'Jon?' she yelled. 'If you're in there, come out. Let Alex go.'

There was no response, not that Danni expected one.

'What do we do?' Leah asked. 'Do we just set fire to the mill as well?' She held up the last bottle of alcohol, giving it a shake.

'No,' Danni said. 'We need to get Alex out.'

Besides, the exterior of the mill was stone, and Danni had no idea how well that would burn. The house behind them, which was turning into a full-on blaze, was timber and was filled with flammable materials that would fuel the flames. But unless the mill had the same amount of junk inside, then the alcohol they had with them in the bottle would be useless.

Danni put a hand to the iron handle and clicked the

latch. The door swung open easily with an audible creak, revealing a thick blanket of unnatural darkness beyond. The faint, flickering glow of the torch barely illuminated past the threshold.

'Alex?' Danni called. No response, at first, but she soon heard a scared whimpering coming, strangely, from a higher plane of space.

She held the torch out before her and stepped inside, feeling the temperature actually drop enough for goose-bumps to break out on her skin. Going by the circumference of the outside of the mill, Danni guessed that the internal floor space—a floor that looked to be timber—was no more than twenty feet in diameter. That wasn't a lot of space, yet the torch didn't give off enough light to see over to the far wall.

Danni was able to see thin timber posts that ran up vertically and knitted together with horizontal ones higher up, forming some kind of frame. Perhaps something left over from its time as a working mill. She looked up farther and heard something that made her blood run cold.

'Mom.'

The voice was weak and came to her just as the light from the torch revealed something.

Up above them, about twelve feet off the ground, was Alex.

He was hanging from one of the horizontal sections of timber strutting. His arms were out to his side, in a position akin to being crucified, and an old, thin rope was tightly wrapped around them, securing him to the wooden bracing. His legs dangled freely and his face was bloodied—looking barely conscious.

'Alex!' she screamed and began to look around frantically for a way up there.

'What should we do?' Leah asked, clinging to Danni's side.

Danni didn't know, but there had to be a way for her to free him.

Before she had a chance to look around for something to aid her, another voice stopped her in her tracks.

'Hi, Danni, glad you came.'

Jon stepped out of the darkness and into her space. Danni didn't have time to act before he smiled and, with one swing of his arm, knocked the torch from her grasp.

She then felt his weight drop onto her and force her to the ground, pinning her down.

'Get off,' she heard Leah yell. 'Dad, stop!'

The torch, still lit, lay just to Danni's side, and she saw her daughter leap onto her father. The girl fought with him bravely and tried to pull him off of Danni, but he just pushed her back with one hand.

With the other, he struck her with a fierce punch.

A horrible crack echoed through the mill. Leah cried out and was sent sprawling to all-fours. Then Danni heard a *clink,* as the bottle Leah had been holding fell to the floor.

Danni exploded with rage and struggled against Jon with renewed vigour, clawing at his face. 'You bastard,' she spat. 'What the fuck is wrong with you?'

At first, Jon seemed taken aback by Danni's ferocity, but he soon managed to overpower her and pin her arms to the floor. He brought his face down to hers, and Danni could see it in his eyes.

This wasn't Jon.

Not anymore.

'Stop,' he said calmly and smiled. His breath smelled of rotting meat. 'I swear to God, Danni, you are making things really difficult. If you don't stop, then it's Leah and Alex who will suffer. Do you understand?'

Danni didn't stop, she continued to squirm and fight. 'How can you do this to your family? You're hurting your kids, Jon, think about what you're doing.'

'I'm not hurting them,' he said. 'I'm saving them.'

'This isn't normal,' Danni went on. 'Did you put Alex up there and bloody his face? Look at him, he's helpless. Jon, think about what you're doing. This isn't you, something else is doing this.'

'I know,' Jon said.

Danni stopped.

'What do you mean?'

'Exactly what I said. I know there is something else doing it. Something greater than us, Danni. And if we don't do what it needs us to, then we'll be destroyed. Torn apart in body and soul. So you see, I'm not lying when I tell you that I'm saving our family.'

Danni was thrown. She had seen the change in him recently, but he'd always been in some kind of denial about what was happening. But now Jon seemed to be fully aware he was being manipulated and was happy enough to go along with it.

'No,' Danni said. 'You aren't saving us. You're condemning us. If you were saving us, you wouldn't have forced us back here. You would have let us go. Hell, you would have come with us, away from whatever this thing is.'

'I can't,' he said, still smiling. 'I admit, it took a while for me to believe this was all real, but, Danni, it's been speaking to me. That thing, it talks to me, and ever since I brought Alex back, I've seen how pleased it is with me. It's shown me things, Danni, things I couldn't have imagined. I've spent my life studying science and the ways of the world, of the universe, but everything I thought I knew was wrong. We, as humans, have no comprehension of how things really work. But I've seen them, Danni, I've glimpsed at a place beyond imagination. Don't you see? Science, religion, any belief system humanity has clung to has been wrong. But I know the truth, and you can too. Can you imagine how powerful that is? How powerful we will be, knowing this, and being aligned with this entity? All we have to do is keep it happy, and it will impart unto us secrets that we could never otherwise know. Just think of all that knowledge, Danni. That truth. We can't say no to that.'

Danni hoped that the man saying this, speaking this madness, was not her husband. That he was just a proxy for the thing behind all of this. Because if any part of the real Jon really meant what was being said, then he was dead to her.

She knew what this thing did to people. She had read the diary and knew that you didn't just align with it.

It consumed you.

'So,' he went on, still smiling, 'do you see now? Do you see why there is no need to run anymore? It will take care of us, we just have to give ourselves over to it.'

Danni was about to answer, but instead she screamed in absolute terror.

Something now stood behind Jon.

She had seen things this weekend that had terrified her; impossible things that made her question her sanity, but the thing that stepped into view now, that stood above Jon looking down at her, shook her to her core and infused her with a sense of terror and dread that she did not think possible.

Her mind could not really comprehend it: both human and not, a twisted waxwork of melted features, both of this world and another. It had dark skin and a bulbous head lined with many, many eyes. Or what she thought were eyes.

It made an inhuman sound, something that bellowed inside of her head.

'Beautiful, isn't it?' Jon said.

'Jon,' Danni cried frantically, 'let me go. Please, let me go.'

She squirmed and fought, and kicked and writhed, but could not break free of his hold.

'There is nowhere to go, Danni. Nowhere else left to run. It lost you once, and it has no plans to lose you again.'

Danni then heard Leah scream as well, but could not see her in the darkness. It was a blackness that actually seemed to permeate from the horrifying creature above her.

The door to the mill slowly glided shut, seemingly of its own accord.

'No more running,' Jon said. 'It's time. It owns us now, and we have to accept that. Give yourself over to it.'

Danni wanted to look away, but couldn't. The demonic thing seemed to bore into her head with its gaze, and she could feel her mind start to break apart.

27

LEAH KNEW her mother needed her.

Her father, if that was really him, had Danni pinned to the floor and was mounted on top of her. The flaming torch that her mother had fashioned was discarded on the floor beside her, allowing Leah to see what was happening. She had briefly seen Alex, suspended high above them, but now he was again lost to the darkness.

However, Leah's horrified attention was fully taken with the vile creature that stood above both of her parents.

She felt like she needed to do something, like she had when the old woman had been choking her mother.

But this? This was different.

The ghostly old woman was terrifying, and it had taken everything Leah had to push herself to act, but the thing that shared the space with them now seemed infinitely more dangerous.

Thankfully, both the monster and her father were focused on Danni. As much as she didn't want to move at all, she knew she now had a chance to escape. Leah knew she could crawl to the door, pull it open, and just run.

But that meant leaving her mother and brother behind. To die.

It was a terrible thought, but what choice did she have? She couldn't fight this. She could do nothing to help her family.

Leah managed to bring her sobbing under control and rolled to her front, looking to the direction she thought the door was in.

She started to crawl forward, one arm in front of the other, focusing on the darkness ahead, not wanting to set eyes on that terrifying thing again.

Leah knew that if she survived, that thing would be in her dreams forever now. Her nightmares. She had no doubt about that. But she would rather live with nightmares and ghosts of the past than confront something that would destroy her now.

It was safer that way.

Leah continued her crawling, trying to keep as silent as possible, focusing her eyes ahead.

As she moved, she felt her hand brush against the bottle she had been holding earlier. She remembered how her mother had used these bottles as a weapon earlier, and Leah paused. She turned her head; no longer able to ignore the struggles that were taking place so close to her. She saw that her mother's head was lolling about and she had begun to scream. Her head fell to the floor and, for a moment, Leah made eye contact with her.

Something was happening. He mother's eyes were rolling back, and she began to bang her head on the floor, as if there were something inside of it causing her pain. But, in that moment when their eyes met, Leah saw so much agony and sadness in her mother's eyes that her own heart broke.

The thought of running away and leaving her mother

and Alex behind wrenched at her gut. How could she do that?

She was still certain that she couldn't help her family. After all, she was only a seventeen-year-old girl. This demon —that possessed her father, and seemed to command the souls of the dead—was so far beyond her, so much more powerful, that going up against it was futile. Anything other than running away was pointless, and a waste of her life.

But she had to help them.

If this act of selflessness was to be her last—and bring about the end of her life—then so be it.

Leah had no real plan, but she had seen how her mother had set the main house ablaze, and how that had seemed to stop the entities in there—enough for the two of them to escape, anyway. An idea formulated, but she would need something to stuff inside the neck of the bottle to hold a flame.

She used her left foot to push the boot off her right, and slid off her sock. The air was biting cold on her bare foot and, as quietly as possible, she unscrewed the top of the bottle, the strong smell of alcohol immediately assaulting her. She quickly jammed the sock into the opening and pushed it farther down with her thumb.

Now, if she could just light the sock she'd have a makeshift weapon. One that could quite easily burn them all alive if things went wrong.

She needed to get to the torch, but in doing so she would be seen—there was no way to avoid that. It was too close to her mother, and therefore too close to her father, and that thing. It would illuminate her to them all. She just hoped she could act quickly enough, and the threat of fire would be enough of a deterrent to give them time to escape.

Leah buried the intense fear down as far as she could

and sprang to her feet, running to the torch. She swiped it up, just as her father, and that thing, turned to her.

She made sure not to look at the monster, only her father, who frowned.

'What are you doing, Leah?' he asked sternly.

Leah held the flame up to the sock, setting it alight. She had no idea how long it would take for the material to burn away, giving the flame access to the golden fuel beneath. 'Let Mom go, Dad. I mean it. I won't let you hurt her.'

'Put that down!' he screamed, his previous, unnatural calm suddenly shattered.

'No!' she shouted back, holding the bottle above her head. 'I won't. I won't end up like one of those things back in the house. I'll burn first.'

'You don't mean that,' her father said and stood up.

'Yes, I do,' Leah said, and she saw her mother roll away, still moaning. Her father held out a large hand.

'Give it to me, girl. Now.'

Leah shook her head. She would not back down.

'Untie Alex and then let us go, then you can have this. But not until.'

'You don't have it in you, Leah. You're a coward, just like your mother. I'm surprised you both didn't run away when you had the chance.'

'Well, we didn't,' Leah said, seeing her mother pull herself to her knees, gulping in air. She seemed shaky and unsteady, however she made eye contact with Leah and gave an almost imperceptible nod.

'We didn't run,' Leah said, holding her father's attention. 'We came back here. And we won't give in to that fucking thing, whatever it is.'

'You don't have a choice.'

Leah saw her mother begin to climb up one of the vertical timber struts, making her way over to Alex.

'Yes, we do. And so did you, but you gave up. We aren't the cowards. You are!'

Her mother climbed higher still, disappearing from the dim light cast from the flame of the bottle and into shadows that actually seemed to swim through the air. The horrible, monstrous thing stood directly behind her father, like a puppet master keeping its toy out ahead to act out its will.

Her father then took a step forward. 'That's a lot of talk,' he said. 'But you still haven't thrown the bottle. And I can see it in your eyes, you look exactly like what you are: a scared little girl.'

Leah raised the bottle higher, genuinely ready to throw it at his feet, but she stopped herself. The man before her had the body of her father, but it wasn't him. It was that thing controlling him. Somewhere inside, her father might still exist. And, if she acted as she wanted to, not only would she put her mother and Alex in danger, but she would also be responsible for killing her dad.

The real man, the one she knew, the one she loved, was a good man. One she was proud to call her father.

This conflict remained unsolved, and it gave him his chance to act. He quickly stepped forward and yanked the bottle from Leah's hand.

'Told you,' he said with a smile and grabbed a handful of her hair. She cried out as he violently shook her head. 'Silly little bitch. You'll learn to do as you're told.'

Leah still had the torch in her other hand, and she wasn't ready to give up just yet. Her father may indeed still be inside there, somewhere, and she knew he wouldn't want her to go down without a fight.

She thrust the torch directly into his face.

Her father screamed and stumbled back in pain. Now free, Leah stepped forward and pushed the fire into his face again.

He floundered, but soon recovered and snatched the torch away from her, quickly plucking it from her grasp. Leah backed up and could smell the faint aroma of burning meat. When her father lifted his head back up with a look of absolute fury she could see raw burn marks bubble on the side of his face.

'I'm going to fucking kill you,' he said, seething.

'Fine,' Leah shouted back, feeling tears start to well up. This was it, she realised. She had failed to protect her family. He was going to kill her now. But at least she had tried. 'Kill me, then. Kill Mom. Kill Alex, too. Kill us all. But just know one thing...'

'And what is that?'

He was snarling, and still holding the torch and bottle. Leah was braced for what was going to happen to her. But, before it did, she had a message for her father.

Her real father.

'That I don't blame you,' she said.

'What?'

'I know you would never do anything like this. I know this isn't you. I want you to know, Dad, if you're in there, that I love you.'

He seemed to stop and cock his head like a confused dog.

'I love you,' she repeated and closed her eyes. 'So, you can kill me now.'

28

JON KNEW he should be attacking his daughter right now.

Killing her.

Just like that thing was commanding him to.

Gut her, destroy her, tear her limbs off. Desecrate her body, if she will not be turned. We have no need for the weak or the wounded. Rip out her throat.

NOW.

But Jon didn't.

He had been slowly losing himself since his arrival at this place without even realising it. Slowly, and unknown to him, this presence had enthralled him, chipped away at him, and taken him piece by piece. It had him now, he knew that, and his real consciousness seemed to exist somewhere beneath all the evil that now surged through his body.

This evil, that had taken Alex and tied him up above them. That had hit Leah and threatened his family. It had used him to do all of these things, while he could only watch. His true self had been suffocated and smothered.

But something changed, if only briefly.

He first felt a flicker of free will stir when Leah had

pushed the flaming torch into his face. The searing pain from the fire burned at his skin, and he felt a sliver of his old self come through. And then Leah's words, so honest and pure, and so heart wrenching, woke him fully, allowing him some measure of control.

But already he could feel his hold weaken again, almost immediately.

The demonic thing would clearly not release its hold.

He could feel it desperately repressing him, pushing him back into that cocoon. But he also knew it was acting quickly, more quickly than it would like—which it had been doing this whole weekend. It seemed time was a factor in fully consuming someone, time the monster did not have, so it acted out of necessity, pushing things too quickly. And maybe if Jon had been exposed for longer, he would have been helpless to rise up no matter what had happened, regardless of what Leah had said.

But right now, there was an opportunity.

He was aware that Danni had climbed the timber structure and was now working to free Alex. The creature knew this too.

It just didn't care.

So sure was it that when Leah was dealt with, it could easily turn its attention to Danni and Alex—to slowly, and steadily, bring them under its control as well.

However, that did not have to be the case. Jon had a few precious moments to act. And, if Danni was quick, then maybe, just maybe, they had a chance.

He was lost to them, he knew that. He'd already felt the thing back inside his mind, putting forward convincing arguments as to why he should tear out Leah's insides and shove them into her mouth as she died.

He knew he didn't have long.

To do what needed to be done.

'Thank you,' he said to Leah.

Then he turned to face the unknowable creature and held the bottle high above his head. He sensed its anger, and it made a move towards him, erupting with a sound born straight from hell.

With the last of his own agency, his own control, Jon turned the bottle upside down and pulled out the material from the neck. This allowed the alcohol inside to run free and over the open flame.

As the liquid poured over him it ignited, like a stream of fire.

The pain hit immediately, and his skin began to burn. He fought against his natural reaction to stop, and let more of the pure alcohol fall from the neck of the bottle, causing more of the fire to spread over him.

He began to scream in agony as it seared and bubbled his skin, burning it away. He heard Leah scream as well, and soon he was fully ablaze.

A human torch.

As well as burning away his skin and slowly stripping him of his life, the purity of the fire also scorched away the hold the creature had over him.

His last moments, as painful as they were, could be filled with unwavering love for his family.

And sorrow. Sorrow for failing them.

But by sacrificing himself he had—hopefully—now given them a chance. He could at least hold on to that.

With the last of his strength, Jon threw himself forward and took hold of the furious creature that had so controlled him. He had been powerless against it before, but his wife and daughter had given him the opportunity, and the strength, to try to make things right. He heard them both scream for him, but there was nothing they could do.

They had already done enough for him.

Their screams sounded far away now, and the thing began to fight back against him. Jon felt its hands pierce through his stomach and pull it open. Still he clung on, letting the blanket of purifying fire wrap over the monster as well.

He thought of his family as his life burned away in a furious, scorching pain.

29

LEAH HAD GIVEN DANNI AN OPPORTUNITY.

Until her daughter's intervention, the monster that controlled her husband had been in her head, probing at her mind.

Pulling it apart.

It was a violation like none imaginable. The things it suggested, the things it wanted her to do—and the way in which it made them seem reasonable—were horrifying. But Leah, yet again, had saved her. The girl, who had been a terrified shell for most of this weekend, had stepped up and saved Danni—twice.

Once free of the horrifying creature's mental torture, Danni acted on instinct and climbed as quickly as she could up the thin frame. She needed to get Alex down, quickly, then bring her kids to safety.

She just hoped that Leah could keep talking Jon down. Already, Danni had managed to get the rope free and Alex, who was only semi-conscious, started to slip from the loose bonds. She had to hold onto him, to keep him from falling.

Then she heard Jon thank Leah.

Before setting himself ablaze.

Danni screamed as she watched her husband burn.

He then moved forward like a human torch and started to wrestle with the thing, holding it back, giving his life to save them. As much as Danni couldn't believe what she was seeing, and as horrifying and heartbreaking as it was watching her husband die, Danni knew she had to act and use the opportunity.

Despite what had happened to him, she knew that Jon, the real Jon, the only man she could ever truly love, was still in there somewhere. And it killed her that she had to try to ignore what was happening to him so she could get her children to safety.

'Mom,' she heard Leah yell up. The girl was wide-eyed, terrified, and had tears streaming down her face. The brave girl now looked so lost, not knowing what to do.

Sickeningly, extra light was afforded by what was happening to Jon, and, what was more, it seemed to be burning away some of the unnatural darkness that hung inside the mill.

'Leah,' Danni yelled down, trying to stay focused in the face of the chaos. 'I need you to catch Alex when he falls.'

'But—'

Danni didn't let her finish, she couldn't let Leah think it through. There was no time for it. She knew the fall might injure Alex, but better an injury than staying here to suffer a similar fate as his father. She pulled the last of the rope free, and Alex fell.

Leah acted quickly, putting her body beneath her brother. She broke his fall as he landed heavily onto her, and the two collapsed to the floor.

Danni leapt down as well, knowing she didn't have time to climb.

She hit the floor hard, and her already injured ankle rolled beneath her again. There an audible snap.

Danni screamed.

But there was no time for pain and certainly no time to acknowledge it. She dug deep, forced herself through it, and pushed herself up. Leah was already getting to her feet, trying to pull up Alex. Danni helped her, and both women took an arm, letting his body rest between them.

'What about Dad?' Leah asked, crying freely.

'We need to go,' Danni said, herself in tears, overcome with all that was going on. She started to move forward, and Leah followed.

Alex was almost a dead weight. He was trying to use his legs, drifting in and out of conciseness, but he was all but limp. Danni tried to take most of his weight, but it was difficult, given her injured ankle, so it was Leah who picked up the slack. The two women dragged Alex to the door, not looking back. Leah reached for the handle and pulled it open, revealing the world outside.

Freedom.

As they crossed the threshold Danni felt Alex pulled from their grasp.

Both girls spun around and saw that ungodly creature backing up to the centre of the mill. Jon's burning body lay slumped on the floor by its feet, and Danni could actually see his insides spilling from his stomach. The demon—or whatever the hell it was—stood at its full, impressive height.

And it had Alex in its arms.

30

DANNI'S HEART felt like it had stopped, and her blood chilled.

The demonic creature that had caused her so much pain throughout her life now had her son in its grasp. The young boy was regaining consciousness now, and a look of horrified realisation dawned over his face as the monster's long hand closed completely around his throat.

After all the misery this thing had caused her: taking her mother, her childhood, turning her father away from her, scarring her for life, and also taking her husband, now it planned to push her over the edge. To take something from her that she could not live without.

It tightened its grip, and Alex began to gurgle.

The vile demon planned to kill one of her children, right before her eyes.

'Alex!' Leah yelled. 'Let him go,' she begged the creature. 'Please, just let him go.'

Danni clenched her fists.

It would not let him go. Whatever this thing was, mercy

and kindness were not in its makeup. The DNA of this demon consisted of hatred, evil, cruelty, and desecration.

Run. Little bitch.

Danni heard the thing speak to her in her mind. As it had before, when Jon had her pinned down. It had whispered things to her as it had torn at her sanity. Now, it was commanding her.

Run away. And always remember how I tore this defective little runt limb from limb. If I cannot have you, then I can ruin you. Now run, and survive in pain and misery until you die, or take your own pathetic life.

Alex's face turned red, and his eyes went wide as the thing applied more pressure.

'Leah,' Danni said quietly to her daughter. 'I need you to do something.'

'Mom—'

'Just listen,' Danni said. She just needed Leah to act when the time was right. The young girl had already saved her twice, and now she needed Leah to get Alex to safety.

And to leave Danni behind.

For there would be no saving her.

This demon—this evil, spiteful thing—would not take her son from her. Danni's children would live on.

'I need to get your brother out of here.'

'Mom?'

'Just do it, baby. You'll know when.' Danni's eyes were full of tears, but she tried to smile through it. 'And don't look back. Just take him and go. And always remember that I love you.'

She put an arm around the confused girl and squeezed her tightly. Danni saw the realisation creep over Leah's face and knew the girl was now figuring out what Danni was planning. Which meant she had to act, before Leah tried to stop her.

Run, you pathetic cunt!

Danni turned back to the demon; the thing that had been a constant evil in her life.

'Fuck you,' she shouted. 'I'm never running from you again.'

Instead, she sprinted towards it.

'Mom!' she heard Leah yell from behind. As she ran, Danni kept her concentration on her son, who was right now fighting for his life.

Once close enough, Danni launched herself forward with a roar and collided into the creature shoulder-first. She felt its arms take hold of her; its grip strong, like iron.

Immovable.

It held her in both hands and twisted her, drawing her back into its cold, bony chest. Though it had her, Danni saw that it had released Alex, who was gasping and wheezing.

Danni lifted a foot and pushed it forward, making contact with her son's backside. She kicked out, forcing him away from her.

Away from *it*.

'Leah!' she screamed as she felt the demon press its large hands around her head. 'Now. Get out of here.'

'Mom!' her daughter cried back.

'Now, Leah!'

Danni felt an incredible pressure on her head, and she let out a cry of pain. She was lifted from the floor by her head and dangled helplessly like a doll.

Die, you wretched bitch.

She ignored the monster as it taunted her. Instead, she called out again as she felt her skull fracture. The pressure building inside her cranium was immense, and the pain agonising.

'Leah... run!'

Thankfully, even though she clearly did not want to, and was crying in fear and heart-wrenching sadness, Leah obliged. She grabbed her brother's arm and pulled him quickly from the mill, practically carrying him over the threshold. Poor Alex was disorientated and weak, and his legs were far more unsteady than normal.

But Leah didn't give up, and she didn't let him stop.

Danni watched as they continued on, away from the dreaded place.

The crushing pain and pressure she felt inside of her head as the demon pressed down harder was becoming unbearable. No matter how much she screamed, it would not let up. The thing would not claim her soul, but in its anger and hatred, it was instead going to take her life.

She heard a crunch and felt an excruciating spike of agony.

The end was here for her now.

Danni was scared. And sad.

Sad that she would never see her husband again, never have him hold her in his arms.

And sad that she would not see her children grow up and would never again tell them how truly and utterly she loved them.

She screamed again as she felt her skull compress. A burst of pressure forced its way through her eye sockets. Danni knew in that last, terrifying moment, that an eyeball had come free.

Still the pain increased.

In her last moments, she prayed for Leah and Alex to carry on and not turn around.

Don't look back, don't look back, don't look back. Keep running.

Her screams were snuffed out as her head collapsed completely.

31

Leah kept going.

She wanted to look back, but even though it took everything she had, she didn't.

She knew that she would be horrified by what she saw if she did.

So she ran, pushing her body, and half-pulling, half-carrying Alex past the blazing house that still burned fiercely, all the way down to the road at the bottom of the drive.

Leah's heart ached.

She was crying almost uncontrollably and wanted to break down.

She knew that by now her mother was dead. Her father too.

Both parents, stripped away from her in the blink of an eye.

By something that should not be real.

How was anyone, let alone a seventeen-year-old girl, ever supposed to come to terms with something like that?

Up ahead, at the end of the long drive, Leah saw the flashing of blue lights against the night sky.

A murmur of voices.

Leah kept going, holding off the impending breakdown she could feel coming. She had to get her brother away from this place for good.

She had to protect him.

'Leah,' Alex said, wheezing. He sounded exhausted. 'Mom and Dad. They...'

He trailed off, and Leah didn't answer. She didn't want to have to tell him about any of that. Not yet.

They broke through to the road, and Leah observed the scene.

She saw their overturned SUV—the family car of a family that was no more—flanked by police cars with blue flashing lights. Officers in high-visibility coats were blocking off the road. Another car, presumably a member of the public, was pulled over to the side of the road. Leah guessed that the driver had come across their crashed vehicle and phoned it in to the police.

'I'm scared,' Alex said, his voice no more than a whisper.

Leah set off again, away from the horror behind them and towards the safety of the flashing lights.

'Help,' she called, her voice croaky and weak. 'Help us.'

The officers turned to face them.

'Help us,' she called again, louder this time, finding her voice. The emotions that she had been suppressing came bubbling out.

'Help us! Help us! Help us!'

She continued to scream it, over and over, and dropped to the floor. She cried, letting everything wash over her. The police moved towards them.

She tried to keep screaming it—*help us*—but her voice

was lost, giving way to hysteria. A blanket was laid over her shoulders, and one of the officers was asking her something.

She could barely hear him.

She continued to cry.

IN THE WEEKS and months that followed, Alex and his sister went through a lot.

After finding them, the police investigated the mill. They found the bodies of their parents, but that was all.

The stories Leah told them about the ghosts, about that demon, were not believed.

Of course they weren't.

The police's best guess was that his mother and father had somehow, for some reason, managed to kill each other. Though they couldn't conclusively prove this.

Alex and Leah went to live with their aunt and her family; a husband and single child.

It was hard.

Leah withdrew.

The experience at Bishops Hill scarred her deeply, and Alex often wondered if she would ever recover.

For Alex, however, it was easier.

The experience had affected him, too, of course, but in a different way.

He remembered being in that mill, hanging helplessly, high up in the dark.

While he did, the thing that lived there spoke to him. Relentlessly.

At first, he resisted it.

But it would not let up. It whispered things to him. Terrible things, awful things.

But in truth, they did not seem awful.

He listened to it.

And, over time, he wanted to hear the thing speak again.

He yearned for it.

And knew that, sometime soon, he would return to Bishops Hill. He would return to what was left of the house, and, more importantly, to the mill.

He would return home.

And he would once again see the demon that called to him.

THE END

THE BRASS FARM MURDERS

If you've read my blog over at www.leemountford.com you will know that I drew inspiration for The Demonic from some real life events.

Whilst this book is an original yarn, some of the history in its back story is based on real life events that happened in my home town of Ferryhill, in the North East of England.

It happened in 1682, on a farm know as Brass Farm—named after the owners; the Brass family. One evening the parents paid a visit to a friends house, miles away, leaving their three children at home.

Alone.

Employed on the farm was a young farm-hand; Andrew Mills, who was known as being a little slow, but harmless. On this night, however, the town of Ferryhill was to see a different side to Andrew Mills.

The parents returned home in the early hours of the next morning to find their three children slaughtered. Reports on how they found Andrew that morning vary—some say he fled, only to be tracked down by authorities, while others say he simply sat outside of the house, waiting for the parents to return home, mumbling about how sorry he was.

His testimony tells of how *something* visited him that night. A monstrous entity, he claimed, got inside his head and demanded that he kill the children. Fearing it was The Devil himself, Andrew took up his axe and chased the children upstairs to a bedroom. They locked themselves in, but he forced his way through the door—breaking the oldest child's arm as he did. Once inside, he set about the two eldest with the axe, concentrating his strikes on their heads and upper bodies. He even cut their throats to stop them screaming.

He then tracked down the youngest girl, someone he considered a friend before this night, who was hiding under a bed. She pleaded with him to spare her life, which seemed to work, and he actually set down the axe and left. But Andrew Mills recounted how the demon visited him again on the landing, telling him; *'Go back, thou hateful wretch, resume thy cursed knife, I long to view more blood, spare not the young ones life.'*

So Andrew returned and—as he put it—*dashed her brains out.*

He was tried and executed, hung in a gib for all to see as he slowly died. His remains were left in the metal cage for a while as they began to rot away.

To his last breath, he maintained that he had been under the influence of a demon (or more precisely, The Devil), who had made him carry out these vile acts.

Whether the Devil played a part or not, what is described above is true and really took place.

The only thing that remains of Brass Farm today is the old corn mill. I've actually been up to it myself, and as kids we used to say that if you ran around it anticlockwise thirteen times—on the stroke of midnight on Halloween—Andrew Mills would re-appear and reenact his heinous crimes. This time on whoever called him back.

Not that this ever happened... that I know of.

But even so, it is interesting to see how much inspiration can be found right there on your doorstep, if you just look hard enough.

So, whilst names and places have been changed for my book (Ferryhill has become Bishops Hill, for example), this was the story behind my character Thomas Kerr and his back story.

As for the character of Margaret Hobbes? I based her loosely on another real life person. Not from my home town this time, but my home county. A woman known as The Dark Angel.

Mary-Ann Cotton.

This woman is thought to have poisoned 21 people over a twenty year period. These consisted of her lovers, husbands and also—sickeningly—her own children.

So, not a nice person!

A bit of a bitch, really.

And those are the inspirations for Thomas Kerr and Margaret Hobbes, which I thought was an interesting thing to share about the book.

As for the demon in the mill? That's all me. Not sure if that is something to brag about though...

- Lee

ALSO BY LEE MOUNTFORD

Horror in the Woods

FINDING THAT DESE-
CRATED BODY WAS ONLY
THE BEGINNING...

For Ashley and her three
friends, it was supposed to be
an adventure-filled weekend.
A chance to get away from the
hustle-and-bustle of city life,
and experience the peaceful
tranquility of nature.

But when they ventured
into those woods, their trip
turned into a horror far
beyond what they could have ever imagined.

Because these four friends have wandered into the terri-
tory of the violent, grotesque Webb family. A group of
psychopaths who have a taste for human meat. And they are
hungry!

Ashley and her friends must face this evil head on, and

worse, discover the shocking secret behind the family's existence...

In the vein of THE EVIL DEAD, TEXAS CHAINSAW MASSACRE, and WRONG TURN - HORROR IN THE WOODS will leave you exhausted and drained. A brutal, violent tale that hurtles along at break-neck pace—one that horror fans should not miss!

THE DEMON OF DUNTON FARM

Enjoy The Demonic?

Find out exactly what happened on that cursed land in Bishops Hill all those years ago, and relive the most grisly events in its history.

The horrifying truth surrounding the demon that dwells on the farm will be revealed in this prequel to The Demonic.

To sign up to my mailing list go to www.leemountford.com and get your free books.

SHORT STORY CONTRIBUTIONS

And now, as a little extra for the people supporting this book, I have the pleasure of including two short stories by some fantastic authors.

First, we have *The Muse*, by Normal Turrell. It is a wonderfully weird horror story with hints of Lovecraft. If you enjoy it (and you will) I highly recommend you check out his other works—they will be well worth your time.

Next up is a deliciously creepy ghost story by Raven Blackwood. Raven is an emerging author of classical ghost stories that will really get under your skin. Her first book, The Haunting of Grove Manor, is coming soon. Be sure to pick it up!

THE MUSE

By Norman Turrell

Gregory was excited about visiting Professor Richards' country home. His last submission to 'Magik and Myth' - 'Angels vs. Demons: Contradictions in Anton LaVey's interpretation of John Dee' must have made a big impression.

The professor's qualifications were astounding. A true polymath. He was known just as well for his mathematical computer art as he was for his contemporary music compositions.

Gregory had first seen him at a Physics lecture at Oxford five years earlier and been entranced by his ability to bring the equations to life. That's when he'd started following the professor's career. In the last two years, there had been distinct change. The professor had suddenly become reclusive and, obscurely, started a magazine devoted to a history of the mystical arts.

His University studies complete, Gregory had been inspired by his idol's latest interest and began to research the same field. His father had recently passed, and the inheritance meant he could indulge himself. He found the study of magics to be greatly engaging; so rich in history, shrouded in secrecy. He spent some time and travel, connecting with magic resources around the world to source novel information.

The drive out of London had been difficult - the motorways always horrendously jammed these days - so the sat nav announcing 'Turn left. In one hundred yards you will reach your destination' was a relief to hear.

Gregory had to duck down to the steering wheel to see up to the towers rising from the professor's classic Georgian home. The sun was getting low and the clear sky above took on a rich, darkening blue.

The car pulled up at the large oak doors and Gregory wondered if he should park it somewhere. His quandary was curtailed as the professor appeared a moment later, opening the door with a smile. He wore tweeds and a jacket, a large book tucked under his arm. Removing his glasses, he waved.

"Gregory," he shouted. "Come in, quickly. This way."

Gregory was taken aback by his friendly manner. They'd discussed a few things over mail, and one abrupt video call about the publication. Nothing as informal as this greeting.

The professor had already disappeared inside. Gregory entered the large hall; a classic of its design with its polished floor and ornate ceiling.

"This way," said the professor. "My office," he added, rushing ahead and through a door to his right.

The office was filled with books and antique curios. The professor was sitting in front of three computer screens and, for the moment, appeared to have forgotten his guest.

Gregory took the opportunity to look around, unwilling to interrupt.

The floor to ceiling bookcase had the items he would expect: large tomes on legends, myths and the occult, both very old and very new. He moved to a glass bell jar containing a black, withered hand, the finger nails yellow, long and sharp. Another contained a straw voodoo doll, complete with pins stuck all over its body, plus one in each eye. A grotesque, wooden mask glared at him from its stand, a painted red tongue hanging down to its chin between pointed fangs.

"Here!" said the professor, pointing to the screen. "It's the last piece. Look." One screen showed an auction website displaying a picture of a half metal coin. "Can you see the inscription?"

The professor scribbled a copy onto a piece of paper and began deciphering it by cross referencing to books laid open on the table. Gregory noticed the table was full of notes and symbols, some with mathematical equations, some accompanied by exquisitely detailed drawings of machines and strange creatures. A white board, standing behind the desk, was filled with the same, their meaning unfathomable to the young man.

He had no idea what the coin was the last part of. As the professor seemed far too busy to ask, he stood by patiently as the man flipped pages and scribbled furiously.

"Excellent," said the professor finally, closing the books and turning to face him, his eyes flashing blue through his spectacles. "Now. You're my next project." His wide, manic smile making Gregory feel distinctly uncomfortable.

"A drink!" shouted the professor as he jumped up, dashing to an occasional table with a decanter of wine. He poured two glasses. "Here. Sit here. No time to lose."

Gregory took his drink and joined the man to sit in two red leather armchairs in front a grand, but unlit, marble fireplace.

"Thank you for inviting me here, Professor," said Gregory, finally finding an opportunity to speak to his host.

"Yes, yes. Of course." The professor reached down to the side of the chair and retrieved a file. He opened it and began mumbling. "Exemplary qualifications... distinction at Oxford. Only child... family deceased. Yes, all in order. Good. Good."

"I beg your pardon?"

"What?" The professor looked up. "Oh, I see. I'm sorry. Please. Drink."

Gregory decided it might be a good idea to still his increasing anxiety and took a swig from the glass.

"Excellent. Now, put the glass down before you pass out."

"What?" said Gregory, already starting to blink to try to clear his vision.

The professor jumped up and grabbed the glass as Gregory's grip loosened. "I don't want my carpet damaged."

The professor stood holding the glass as the young man slumped in the seat.

Gregory woke, immediately aware of the tape over his mouth. He pulled at the ropes fastening his wrists and ankles securely to his seat. His shirt had been removed and, as he struggled, he looked rapidly around the room, lit only by candles. The professor wore a black, ritual robe. He held a large, leather bound book open in one hand, waving the other, all the time half muttering, half singing strange words. Gregory tried to speak and struggled harder, but the chair itself was secured to the floor.

There was a humming sound - a building resonance - that permeated his body. It made his head buzz. The room itself seemed to be shaking, vibrating, the walls appearing to blur. The professor closed the book and stared at the wall in front of Gregory.

The wall appeared to bulge outward in several places, in a way impossible for stone to behave, then return. There was a sudden cracking sound as a split appeared at the top, the rent following a jagged course, like a lightning bolt, to the floor. The gap began to separate, fingers squeezing through the crack. Long, thin fingers, extended by red painted nails. Two hands were now visible. The skin was ashen grey, stretched tight across bone and sinews. Where the light from the candles caught it, it shone like moonlight. They strained to increase the opening.

There was a hiss as the crack gave way further, and a sweet, flowery smelling mist poured into the room, flowing across the floor. Gregory's eyes were wide, fixed on the show before him.

A foot wiggled through the base of the crack - a ballet slipper - followed by a leg covered in a long white skirt of lace fabric. A body forced through sideways, eager to be through the opening, only just wide enough for the thin frame. Finally through, a woman stood before them, her hair waist length, straight and black. Her face was flawless, but with skin like her hands, shining bright. Her eyes were ovals of black and her mouth twisted into a wicked, red-lipped smile.

"Muse," said the professor, beaming with delight at her success in entering the chamber.

"Matthew. My sweet mad scientist. Not totally insane

yet?" She shook herself and smoothed back her hair. She looked at Gregory staring at her. "Surely you can't mean to offer another?"

She wandered over to Gregory and trailed her nails over his bare chest, the razor sharp tips leaving dripping trails of red behind them. She looked back to Matthew.

"Your struggle against the inevitable is a delight. I love it when my creatives lose their senses. You know this can't go on, Matthew. You can't absorb anymore intellect, even though I adore the empty shells it leaves me. So... malleable."

"But... but I need more. The things I have discovered from your gifts. I'm so close to unlocking such mysteries. Take this one. See what I'll achieve, in your name."

The muse looked back to Gregory and leant her face close to his. He felt her breath, smelt its faintly sweet scent. Her jet black eyes scanned across his forehead and cheeks. She sniffed his hair, puzzling at some unknown perception, then settled to stare deep into his eyes. Gregory's body deflated, the muscles relieved of all tension, his eyes and face relaxing. The muse stood back slowly. She flicked her hand and the ropes binding Gregory to his seat burst into flames for an instant, then were ash.

"I like this one. He's got potential." Her head swung round, and she fixed the professor in her sight. "You're done, Matthew. Time to move on."

"No! I must-"

Another wave from the muse and the professor's protestation was silenced. She held out both hands and a shaft of glowing light struck his forehead. The other hand raised, and an identical beam hit Gregory. Her eyes grew bright, shining with the same glow. The three figures stood transfixed until, abruptly, the display concluded. She pointed towards the wall and the professor walked forward in a trance, his body fading from view as he reached it.

"I'll be seeing you," said the muse, smiling and winking at Gregory, before walking to the wall herself.

Gregory completed his calculations with a smile, leaning back to enjoy the comfortable chair and his new offices. He closed a web page, heralding his award winning debut at the Cannes film festival, to answer an insistent video call.

"Hello, professor," said the young woman on the screen, her red hair tied back. Behind her glasses, her green eyes exposed of her nervousness.

Gregory looked down at a manuscript on his desk and then back to the woman. "Thank you for sending me your work, Alice. I was very impressed with your screenplay. A unique insight into the human condition. Very innovative."

The woman blushed visibly. "Thank you. That means a lot to me, coming from you. I'm such a fan of your work."

"I'd really like to work with you. I wonder if you could fill out the online personal information form - just a formality for my lawyers - and then, perhaps, we could meet?"

About Norman Turrell:

Norman is a commercial writer/editor and best-selling Amazon author of science-fiction, fantasy, horror and just strange stories. He blogs on Huffington Post, produces printed local publications, runs live writers critique groups and is a member of many online writing communities.

He studied Mathematics at college, obtaining a 2.1 Hons and later a MSc (Merit) in Artificial Intelligence.

In his spare time he runs a ukulele group and reads as much as he can. He also has a full time job as a Software Department Manager, which includes programming systems in C++.

Full information on all his activities, including some dabbling in photography and art, can be found at www.normanturrell.com - with a free gift as thanks to all who register.

Publications:

Alice in Virtuality : An adventure in the real... and the not so real : myBook.to/AliceInVirtuality

Martin, an anti-social and reclusive computer programmer, is dragged into an adventure which spans the real world and the virtual when he loads an artificial intelligence program called 'Alice'. Pushed into action as the program attacks his life, he teams up with others who are affected in an attempt to defeat the menace - but how? Alice is everywhere.

Points Of Possibility : A collection of sci-fi, fantasy and horror short stories : myBook.to/PointsOfPossibility

Ranked #1 Best Seller in two categories (UK rankings Sept. 2016)

A collection of nine short stories from the imagination of best selling British author, Norman Turrell, ranging from science fiction, fantasy, horror and purely strange tales.

THE HAUNTING OF ELDERFIELD HALL

By Raven Blackwood

Prologue

1910, Elderfield Hall, Upper Merton, Berkshire.

The child fell, twisting, tangled in her skirts, and two screams echoed through the vaulted space of the grand entryway.

Mimi screamed in her mind, as well as with her voice 'Nooooo' – they always fought, always had, but this time, somehow, the push and shove had gone too far, and now Ella was gone from in front of her, tumbling helplessly down the long curving stairs.

The two screams intertwined, so sharp that they seemed to penetrate the whole space, saturating the air with terrible sound. Then, a harsh 'thump' and one scream stopped, cut off sharply, leaving the remaining sound somehow thinner, shredding into a wail of horrified despair.

Ella lay at the foot of the stairs, her skirts about her like the petals of some giant flower, her head at a grotesquely wrong angle. Rushing footsteps echoed on the marble floor. Then stopped. After a moment, a voice, flat and frightening, spoke.

"Oh Mimi, what have you done!" The long wailing scream went on, soaking into the house, seemingly unaware of the voice, almost as if detached from everything.

The woman dropped to her knees beside the fallen child, with a strangled sob.

"Ella, Ella, please, please be alright." Even as she spoke, she knew it was not to be – the child's neck was quite obviously broken, her heart and breathing stopped forever. She gathered the broken child in her arms, and walked from the hall, ignoring her other child and the still echoing wail of despair.

Within the week they were gone, the house closed up, her memories of those moments locked inside. She refused to speak of it, and her grief made her odd and detached. She refused to speak to Mimi, leaving her husband to deal with the girl. He hoped it might get better, given time, but it never did. Mimi, convinced that her mother hated her, hated herself as well, and no amount of loving care from her father could change that.

The mother faded away, her will to live gone, the father faded with her, his vitality drained by the double grief of the loss of his child, and of his wife. By the time she was fifteen, they were both gone, and Mimi was alone. She made a choice. She would stay alone. She would not marry, she would not bear a child – she would never again put another person she cared about in a position where she could hurt them.

Chapter One

Izzie opened the door with the antiquated brass key, and stepped inside. Puffs of dust rose from the floor with each step. Sneezing, she deposited the cat carrier on the floor near the imposing staircase and looked around. Beaufort released an offended yowl, and batted at the door of the carrier.

"Not yet, Beau, not until I make a good place where you'll be safe in this great monstrosity of a house!"

Monstrosity was right! She was still in shock at the size of it.

When she'd first received the letter from a legal firm, requesting her presence at the reading of a will, she'd been half inclined to think it some sort of scam – but a bit of investigation had proven that they were legitimate, so she'd gone. From there, it just got stranger – she hadn't really believed in that Law of Attraction stuff, but in this case, it did seem like the universe was providing for her. She'd had, at that point, precisely a week's worth of money in the bank, a lease on her ratty little flat that ran out in precisely that week, and no way to extend it, nowhere else to live either.

She couldn't be in any way sorry that Ralph was out of her life, but she sure as hell was sorry that he'd emptied the bank accounts before he'd had the courtesy to leave the country. Her freelance job paid OK – when she had clients, which, right now, she didn't – so, no money. When the lawyer explained that she had a great aunt, once removed, by the name of Jemima Winterford, she had been stunned. Izzy had vaguely known that her mother's cousins' family was called Winterford, but that was about it.

She had been even more stunned when she was told

that she was the only female child in the extended family, in her generation, and that her great aunt's will specified that everything go to her. Everything included a moderate amount of money, most of which was well invested, so not so easily accessible, and this house. A house that her great aunt had not lived in since she was a child, but which she had never sold. A house that hadn't even been rented out for more than 20 years. The woman had been 96 when she died, and had spent the last 20 years in a retirement home. Apparently, there was some more money to come from the housing bond release on that – but that could take a while to arrive.

It looked like the place hadn't been cleaned in that 20 years – what a job she had ahead of her! Still, what choice did she have? Until more cash arrived (if it actually did) she couldn't afford anywhere else to live – she owned this, however run down it was, so it cost her nothing but patience and some cleaning effort to make it liveable.

She shivered, realising that it was very cold where she stood, as she thought about it all, which was odd, given it was midsummer, and quite hot outside. Izzy shook herself out of her musings, and picked up the cat carrier, to another disgruntled yowl from Beau, and set off to explore further. She shivered, but ignored the cold as she went past the stairs towards the back of the house – the most likely place for such critical things as a kitchen!

Once that was found, she would unload her pitiful collection of belongings from the car, and settle in.

Chapter Two

"Beau – no! That is not a toy for you to chase!"

Izzy retrieved the cleaning cloth from the ginger cat's

claws, and returned it to the pile on the sink. The cat huffed at her in typical cat fashion, and settled to sleep on the one decent chair at the table, with an expression which was meant to convey 'I didn't really want it anyway'. Izzy wasn't fooled.

She blew an escaped strand of her red gold hair out of her eyes and surveyed the room. The kitchen now actually looked like a place where you might prepare food. The little microwave oven she'd bought looked outrageously modern and out of place in the classic country house style kitchen, but she didn't care. Warm food was a necessity. For now, she only had a tiny bar fridge and the microwave to make meals possible – the original wood stove looked wonderful – but a careful chimney cleaning would be needed before she dared light it.

So, that made three rooms restored to useability – the kitchen, the downstairs bathroom (which was also anti-quated – it could look good, in that 'historic style' but she wanted it to be more modern underneath that... And right now, it only just passed for useable – and the bedroom she was using – which she suspected had once been a house-keeper's room, as it was close to the kitchen and fairly small. She had barely explored the rest of the house, she'd been so focused on making this small part liveable. That was tomor-row's agenda – explore, and decide what to tackle next.

Wandering into the hallway, she looked around at the grand entry, the elegant curved stairs dominating the space, and tried to imagine it in its heyday, 100 years or more ago. She imagined so hard that, for a second, she could almost see a young girl, dressed in early 1900's clothes, standing at the top of the stairs, looking down. She shook her head at the whimsy, and turned away to consider the doors to either side – perhaps she would start with one of the front rooms tomorrow – they seemed to be sort of parlour / lounge room type spaces – having a place to relax might be a good next step.

As she turned, she caught, again, that flicker of movement at the top of the stairs – crazy – there was nothing there. Moving forward to the parlour door, she stepped past the end of the stairs and a wave of chill enveloped her. She shivered, surprised, wondering if she was catching something – it was a warm day, and she'd felt almost overheated a minute ago. The sensation passed as she reached out to open the door, and she shrugged off the oddity.

The room behind the door was beautiful, half-timber panelled and wallpapered in an art deco type pattern that would cost a fortune to get today. The old furniture was, surprisingly, not so much coated in dust – in places it almost shone. Definitely the place to start tomorrow. She could just imagine herself relaxing in here with a nice warm fire in the hearth – once the chimney was cleaned...

There was a painting above the carved mantelpiece – a family portrait – a man and woman in their twenties or early thirties, with two young girls – maybe 4 and 5 in age. Their clothes suggested the Victorian era, and they looked so happy it made her smile. She wondered who they were – some far distant relatives of hers, perhaps? Was her great aunt Jemima one of those girls? She supposed she'd never actually know. Satisfied with her plan for the morning, Izzy headed back into the hallway, planning on a nice warm cup of tea before bed.

As she stepped through the door, it slammed behind her, before she could even touch it, and suddenly she was chilled all over again. Maybe there was a crack somewhere letting in a cold wind? Maybe that's why the door had slammed? But where? She shivered, and hurried back to the kitchen, and the reassuring company of the cat.

Chapter Three

Izzy normally slept well – she wasn't prone to insomnia, nor to bad dreams, and the daily effort in cleaning the place made sure that she was tired enough to sleep. Snuggled under her doona, with Beaufort curled up against her, she drifted off to sleep, looking forward to working on that delightful parlour in the morning.

She wasn't sure, at first, why she was awake – for a few seconds she had no idea where she was, then memory returned – the house, the whole strange thing that was her life right now. Then it sunk in that she was hearing something - something odd. A high-pitched sound that grated on her, a faint wailing noise, almost like someone screaming in the distance.

She shivered, wondering what it was, suddenly deeply conscious of being alone in a very big old house, in a town she didn't know, with no-one for company but a grumpy cat. The sound went on, and Beau sat up, staring into the darkness, his fur all ruffled, his ears laid back. He hissed.

Izzy was startled – he never hissed. Should she get up and investigate? But... she found that idea distinctly unappealing – part of her didn't want to know...

Berating herself, she dragged herself up – she was a strong modern woman – what the hell was she doing? Waiting for some guy to come and deal with it for her? What a load of rubbish! Time for her to get over herself and move.

Pulling a dressing gown around her, she headed in the direction of the sound, turning on every light as she went.

She had been startled to discover that all of the electrics in the place worked – now she was very grateful that they did. Beau stalked along beside her, his tail all fluffed up, and a little rumbly growl in his throat. That did absolutely nothing to reassure her.

The sound seemed to be coming from the hall, the entry way area somewhere and her steps slowed as she got closer. Oddly, it didn't seem to be getting any louder – there was just, somehow, a sense of direction about it.

She stepped into the hall, and, as she got closer to the entry way, to the foot of the stairs, the air became steadily colder. She shivered, feeling like the sound was penetrating her bones, reaching icy fingers deep into her.

Chapter Four

Izzy stood near the wall, looking around, as she reached out and turned on the main lights in the vaulted entryway space. As the lights came on, she saw, again, that flicker of movement at the top of the stairs, and the chill intensified.

But the second that the lights were on, the sound stopped – it was as if the light switch had turned it off, click, just like that, when it turned the lights on. The chill faded fast from that moment, and Izzy was left standing in the empty hall, staring at the empty stairs, and feeling a bit foolish.

Still – for the first time since Ralph had taken her for everything and run off with Jewel West to live in Thailand, she was not so keen on being alone. Having someone for company seemed, right at that moment, like a very good idea.

Beau had stopped growling, and was sitting at her feet, grooming, making sure that all of those tail hairs that had been fluffed up were laid back in EXACTLY the right place. Once sure that they were, he picked himself up and headed back down the hall, giving her a look over his shoulder that obviously said 'Are you coming back to the bed?'.

All the damned cat cared about was having a warm human to snuggle up against. It was then that she noticed the little side window near the front door – it was ajar – and a breeze fluttered the ragged curtain as she watched. She let out her breath in a rush – there was the explanation, surely – a breeze through the window creating both the sound and the impression of movement. She felt like a complete idiot.

She shut and latched the window firmly and took herself back to bed, turning off all the lights as she went.

The following morning, in the clear light of day, it all seemed beyond silly, and Izzy set about her cleaning, determined to not be so fluff-headed in future. The front parlour really was beautiful, and she suspected that the old furniture might, itself, be worth a fortune on the antiques market, but she loved the room, she wouldn't sell it.

After a few hours, it looked gorgeous, sitting in there was almost like stepping back in time. She sank to the couch, pleased when no puff of dust resulted, and looked up at the painting in front of her. Again, she was struck by how happy they looked. She wondered if they really had been that happy, or if the artist had simply made the painting flattering. She hoped they had been happy.

Her musings were interrupted by a knock at the door – she jumped in surprise – she knew no one in the town, so who could it be?

On the doorstep stood one of the staff from the legal

office.

"Ms Landers?"

"Yes, how can I help you?"

"Mr Felton asked me to bring you this."

He proffered a large cardboard carton.

Izzy took it, carefully, looking at him with a raised eyebrow.

"What is 'this'?"

"Ah, it's some things from old Miss Winterford's rooms at the retirement home. Apparently, she had things hidden away in every crevice she could find – you know how old people get as their minds start to wander. The ladies cleaning out the rooms found a couple of boxes and bits and pieces tucked right away at the back, way under the bed against the wall. As everything of hers goes to you, these do too. I have no idea if they have any value or interest to you, but I'm legally bound to give them to you."

Izzy nodded and smiled at the man – this could be interesting – she might get some better idea of what her great aunt had been like.

"Well, thank you for bringing them."

"Not a problem Miss, good day to you then."

He took himself off, obviously glad to have the errand done with, and Izzy took the box inside, kicking the door closed behind her, and settled back in the parlour to examine what was in there.

The box proved to contain a scatter of things – mostly predictable items like bits of jewellery, faded photos of unknown people, odd little bits of embroidery and more. But one item stood out. A small wooden chest – the sort of thing that people used to keep their personal keepsakes and precious items in. The chest was wooden, carved sandalwood if she wasn't mistaken, probably made in China or Malaya and horribly expensive when her great aunt had been young.

It was locked, and there seemed to be no key. Izzy blew the ever-escaping lock of hair out of her eyes and studied it. How could she open it? It had an odd metal lock on a pin and hasp closure – she had never seen anything quite like it. But maybe, just maybe, she could pick the lock. There was no obvious hole for a 'normal' key anyway – perhaps she just hadn't worked out how the thing operated yet.

Trying to be logical, she picked the cardboard carton up and upended it, just in case she had missed something, some other item, or even a key. A piece of paper fluttered out. She shook it. Something small dropped to the floor, and rolled to one side. In a flash, Beau was on it, batting it away and chasing it across the room.

Izzy dropped the box and chased him.

"Beau, give me that! No, you damn cat, it's not a chasing game, give me that thing!"

Five minutes, one scraped arm, and the grime from the underside of a sideboard that she obviously hadn't cleaned well enough, and Izzy was the proud possessor of an odd little cylindrical thing, and a thoroughly unimpressed cat.

She collapsed on the couch and studied the odd little object. Could it be a key? Maybe. A few minutes fiddling about proved that it was, indeed a key, fitting into the strange metal lock like a puzzle piece. She dropped the lock onto the small table beside the carved box and paused.

For some reason, she was almost scared to open it – what might she find inside? Beau jumped up onto the table and sat, staring at the box. He sniffed at it, then shook his head with a loud cat sneeze. Izzy laughed and reached out to open the lid.

As soon as she touched it, she felt cold – ice cold, her fingertips burning as if she really was touching ice. She made herself continue, lifting the lid carefully. Inside the box were two small necklaces, and a leather-bound book.

She looked at the necklaces – they seemed ordinary enough – little lockets in an old-fashioned style, intricate gold work on thin gold chains. The book was more interesting – what might it tell her of her great aunt's life?

Chapter Five

The book was a journal, a diary of sorts, and a quick flip of the pages showed a vast difference in the writing through the length of the book – it looked like this had been written in over many, many years. At the beginning, the hand was that of a very young child, all uneven and wobbly. But the words grabbed Izzy and shocked her deeply, dragging her in to read, unable to stop herself.

'I hate myself. I'm supposed to. My mother hates me now too, but she should, given what I did. Father tries to be nice to me, but I know he must be just hiding how he feels. How could he not hate me too?'

As she read, the air around her chilled even further, and she shook. Beau hissed at her, jumped off the table and went to the other side of the room. What could make a young child write such things? She read on, shaking from the cold, but unable to stop. Each page revealed more horror, from the tragic death that the child believed she was wholly responsible for, to the self-hatred that had consumed her.

How could parents allow a child to suffer so, to believe such things? Yet, perhaps the child was right, perhaps the parents believed it too. Which was another layer of horror again. Was the child writing this her great aunt? Had she lived her whole life with this great guilt?

Izzy found herself crying, unable to stop, and kept reading, heartsick at what was on the pages, colder and colder for every page she read and, steadily, more and more scared.

A sound distracted her – she looked up, and dropped the book. The little necklaces were moving – rattling about in the sandalwood box, all by themselves. She leapt up and, as she did so, her eyes went to the portrait. The two little girls in the portrait were wearing necklaces identical to the ones in the box. And the faces in the portrait no longer looked happy...

Izzy ran from the room, Beau scooting past her as she ran out the door, slamming it after her. She didn't stop until she was in the kitchen, her heart racing, her face still wet with tears.

She sank onto the chair, scooping up Beau and hugging him to her. He purred, and licked the tears off her face. She had never believed in all that supernatural stuff, but... What had just happened? Jewellery didn't just move about by itself, and century or so old paintings didn't change in front of you. But... they just had.

Was she crazy? Or, scary, scary thought, was there actually really something to all that supernatural stuff after all? What was she going to do? Sure as hell, she didn't want to go back into that room! She wasn't even sure she wanted to be in this house right now. There wasn't much choice though – where else could she go?

She had very little actual cash, and no other options but here. OK then. She wouldn't let this beat her. Izzy deposited the cat on the floor, wiped the last of the tears from her face, and got herself a coffee. Her brain was going around in circles – what had she seen? Was it real? How could she find out for sure?

And, on top of all that, she wanted to read the rest of the journal. She had to know more about the life that was written in those pages, she wanted to know, for sure, if it was her great aunt Jemima who had written it. The terrible words of the young child echoed around and around in her thoughts, and she couldn't let go of the sense of horrific despair they held. But reading more would mean going back into the parlour...

Chapter Six

She woke the next morning still tired. She hadn't slept well, and had dreamed – terrible dreams where she floated through the empty house, surrounded by an eerie wailing cry that wouldn't stop. The fog of the dream cleared slowly from her mind, and she only dragged herself up when Beau made it very clear that he needed to go outside... NOW!

Izzy spent the morning exploring more – she walked through the upstairs rooms, where furniture was covered in dust sheets and everything looked like it hadn't been touched for more than the 20 years the place had been empty. But the sun through the dirty windows was warm, and the light was enough to let her imagine what the place might look like, all cleaned up. It was enough to motivate her to keep cleaning.

In the soft warm sunlight, her fears of the previous day seemed silly – surely she had imagined all that with the painting? Well, she decided, she wanted to read more of that journal, so there was nothing for it – she was going back into the parlour to do just that. On impulse, she grabbed one of the dust sheets and took it with her – there was one way to stop the sensation of the painting watching her. She was just going to cover it up!

When she reached the top of the stairs, the sharp chill surrounded her again, and she shivered, wondering if the temperature in this house could ever be managed. The cold stayed with her, getting stronger as she reached the bottom of the stairs, and more so when she entered the parlour.

She went immediately to drape the cloth over the painting, in which the people looked innocently happy again – had she imagined it all? Turning, she stopped, and a sharp knife of fear slid into her. The book, which she had dropped to the floor when she fled the room, was sitting in the box, leaning on the necklaces, neatly propped open at the last page she had read.

How did it get there?

Izzy stood, shaking, then forced herself forward. She was going to read it, no matter what.

An hour later, shivering from the freezing cold, Izzy was still reading. So far nothing untoward had happened, apart from the unnatural cold. It was so heartbreaking to read! The child had a miserable life, was utterly consumed with her sense of guilt, and was ignored by the mother she so desperately wanted to feel loved by.

She had reached the point where the girl described her mother's death, and the aching emptiness it left in her, then, not long after that, her father's rapid decline in health, and his eventual death. When she read the part where the girl described her last conversation with her father, she was overwhelmed with sorrow.

'Father lay there, all thin, and pale and barely able to breath. He looked at me with his big sad eyes, and then forced himself to speak.

"Mimi, I'm so sorry, I never wanted to leave you like this. I

tried to make your life good, but I know I have failed you in so many ways. Your mother failed you too, but she didn't know how to do anything else. Here, take this..."

He held out a large sealed envelope. It had my name on it, written in Mother's handwriting. I took it, not sure that I wanted it.

"she wrote that for you, before she died. She told me to give it to you, once you were old enough to understand. I don't know if that's now, but this is the last chance I'll have to give it to you. I love you Mimi, no matter what happened."

He closed his eyes, and drifted away. He never woke up again.

I looked at the letter in my hand. I wasn't going to read it. Ever. I have locked it away – what could she have to say, that I would want to hear? Anything would be too little to make a difference, and so many years too late.'

Izzy was crying again, tears running down her face, her sobs echoing in the room. Wait... was that an echo... it sounded like... like someone else crying... in the hallway?

The book dropped from her shaking hand, but somehow landed neatly beside her, still open at the page she had been reading. Izzy froze, for the first time truly terrified. She was too scared to read more, too scared to leave the room, for that would mean going into the hallway – the hallway where _someone else_ was crying...

Sitting there, unable to do anything, made it worse, frantic, Izzy paced about the room, still crying, from fear now, physically shaking, she glared at the book lying on the couch. It was as if it wanted to be read, as if it knew where she was up to, and made sure to be open at that page! The thought was the last straw, it tipped her over the edge and into action, suddenly the book seemed more sinister than even the crying in the hallway.

She fled the room. The door slammed behind her, all by itself. As her feet touched the marble of the hall floor, the space around her filled with sound – three voices screamed and sobbed, intertwined, seeming to permeate the walls, the air, her every cell. What did they want?

The elegantly curved staircase seemed the centre of a whirlwind of terrifying sound. She clapped her hands over her ears, sobbing helplessly herself, and, as she stared at the curving rise of steps, realised, with horror, that *this* staircase was the one described in the book – this was where the tragic death of the other child had happened – right here in her house!

Later, Izzy had no memory of running, she just found herself outside, in the back garden, desperate for the warmth of the sun on her skin and the normal sounds of the world around her. What could she do? She had nowhere else to go, but how could she stay here, in a house that, it seemed, was very much occupied by ghosts?

Chapter Seven

Another night of little sleep and terrifying dreams left Izzy worn and still very scared. And no closer to a solution. She couldn't live like this, but she had no other options. The last part of the book that she had read nagged at her thoughts – it was as if the ghosts, if that's what they were, knew what she was reading, as if that was what had started the whole sobbing and wailing thing.

She wondered why. She also, when she considered the way she was thinking, wondered about her sanity. Here she was, thinking as if ghosts were real, and in her house!

But... what if they were? What did they want? Why were

they still here, and not gone wherever most dead people went? Maybe she'd never know.

The other thing that nagged at her thoughts, was the letter from Mimi's mother, described in that last bit she'd read. Had Mimi ever read it? What did it say. Izzy wanted to know. And the only way she would maybe find out, was to read more of that damned journal!

Which she was not going to do, in that room, again. No way. But – maybe if she took the book out into the garden – could ghosts come outside? She didn't know. But it was worth a try. Izzy took a deep breath, spoke to herself sternly, and almost ran through the hallway, into the parlour, grabbed the book (which was, as expected, sitting there open at the last page she'd read, waiting for her...) and ran back out, all the way to the garden before stopping.

In the garden, the icy chill from the book wasn't so bad, and she found that she could handle reading it. By late afternoon, she had read almost to the end. It was, by then, very obvious that Mimi was her great aunt Jemima (it was a logical shortening of the name, when she thought about it), and that, sadly she had never read the letter.

Izzy couldn't imagine keeping something like that for 80 years or more and not reading it! But, apparently, the old woman had – her bitterness and guilt had run that deep. Sadly, towards the end of her life Jemima had decided that she would read the letter after all, but had been unable to find it. There were no clues in her diary as to where she had hidden it – only that she had put it away somewhere 'safe' when she had first moved to the retirement home, and then, with the failing memory of her last years, not known where it was anymore.

A crazy idea occurred to her. What if she could find the letter? What if it was till somewhere at the retirement home, and they just hadn't found it? Izzy picked up the book and went back inside.

~

The dreams were less that night, as if having read more had somehow helped, but they were still there. If this kept up, she might never feel rested again.

First thing in the morning, she rang the lawyers and got the name of the retirement home. Calling them, she felt a bit idiotic, but they seemed understanding about her concern that something of her great aunt's may still be hidden somewhere – after all, the old woman had hidden things all over the place. They agreed to search the rooms again.

Izzy sat in the sun on the garden bench, holding the book, and thinking about it. The last pages, whilst the writings were rather rambling, as was to be expected from a very old person, somehow conveyed the feeling that Jemima regretted everything in the end – not reading the letter, not reconnecting with her mother in any way, not having any way to get over her guilt about Ella's death.

There were even short sections of the writing where Jemima seemed to be talking to Ella, and to her mother, trying to tell them how she felt. Perhaps, just perhaps, that was what this was all about? Were the three of them – Mimi, Ella and their mother, her ghosts? Somehow, that thought made it a little less terrifying, for, through the book, Izzy felt like she had come to know them in a way.

On impulse, and before she could think too much about it and get afraid, she picked up the book and went to stand at the foot of the stairs. Beau followed her, curious, and plopped down beside her, staring intently at the bottom stair. Izzy took a very deep breath, and feeling a bit ridiculous, started to speak.

"Mimi, Ella, Mrs Winterford, are you here? Is it you who screamed and sobbed at me yesterday?"

There was no sound, but the air around her chilled so fast that she was surprised her hair hadn't got icicles on it. Izzy began to shake – it was one thing to think about the possibility of ghosts, it was another entirely to be talking to them.

"I've read your story, Mimi, I know that you couldn't find the letter, when you at last wanted to read it. Mrs Winterford, I think, maybe, you're still here because you want so much for Mimi to read it."

A light breeze lifted Izzy's hair, and the chill got stronger. Beau fluffed up his tail and kept staring at the steps. Around her, the hallway echoed with soft sobbing – no screams this time, just heartbreaking despairing crying.

"I will find the letter if I can, I will try to help you."

The sobbing continued, but the chill lifted, and Izzy had the most disconcerting sensation, as if a hand touched hers.

Chapter Eight

Izzy slept well, for the first time in days, and woke with renewed energy for cleaning and restoring her house. When she stopped in the late afternoon, her phone rang, and she grabbed it hopefully. With any luck, it might be a client with a job for her – some cashflow would be very welcome right now!

Instead, it was the retirement home. They had found something – what seemed to be a very old packet of letters, wrapped in oilskin, which was tucked in behind a crack in the back panelling of the wardrobe in aunt Jemima's room.

For a moment, the room spun around Izzy – this was way more than she had expected, so fast – and it was wonderful – maybe it even was 'the letter'! The people at the home were sending it over by courier right away.

An hour later, as the darkness closed in on the house, she stood in the hallway, holding the oilskin packet. Unfolding it carefully she laid aside a collection of clippings and other papers, putting them down on the hall table beside the book, and looked at the envelope in her hand.

"Mimi, Ella, Mrs Winterford? Are you here? I have the letter."

The breeze lifted her hair, and the air chilled almost immediately. The air around her shimmered, as if there was something there, that she couldn't quite see.

"I'm going to open the letter now."

Izzy started as invisible hands touched hers, patted her hair, patted her back. She split the old seal on the envelope, careful with the crackly dry old paper, and unfolded the letter. It was short, written in a hand that was a little shaky, as if the person who had written it was very weak. She began to read.

"My dear Mimi, I am so very sorry – for everything. It is only now that I am close to death that I can see and think clearly. It's as if Ella comes to me when I dream, and sometimes when I wake, and talks to me. She tells me not to blame you, that she doesn't, she loves you, like she always did, and so should I.

She is so wise. She reminded me that the two of you always fought, just like most siblings, and that in any fight, both of you could be said to be at fault. So, if anyone is to blame for her death, it's her as much as you – if she hadn't fought with you, she wouldn't have been in a place where she could fall.

I wish I could have spoken to you again before I die, but you wouldn't come. I suppose I deserve that, after the way I have treated you. So please, understand that I am so, so, sorry, I do love you, and I hate myself for what I have done. Please, if you possibly can, forgive me, and live the best life you can. Ella will come for me soon, and I am ready to go.

Love Mother."

Izzy stopped, and looked up at the stairs, her eyes filled with tears. At first, nothing happened – the room stayed cold, and silent. Then, like a shimmery reflection in her tears Izzy saw something. Out of the empty air at the top of the stairs, the translucent figure of a girl, dressed in century old clothing, appeared.

She smiled, and walked down the steps. As she neared the bottom, another two figures materialised – another girl nearly the same age, and a woman, holding out her hands to both of them.

Izzy was frozen in place, amazed at what she saw, still crying, but happy tears now.

The ghost woman took the hands of both ghost children, they all smiled at Izzy, then turned and walked away right through the hall table and the book resting on it, fading out as they did so. The chill in the air went with them, and the room filled with warmth, and the scent of spring flowers.

The book opened, all by itself, to the last page.

On the page of the book, writing appeared, beautiful script which looked like the writing in Jemima's hand in her mid-twenties, scrolling onto the page as if an invisible pen wrote there.

'Goodbye Isabella, godchild, descendant of my heart, our blessings and thank you'

Followed by Jemima's signature.

Izzy stared at it in wonder, then gathered up the book and the papers, and went into the parlour to uncover the painting. It was right that they see the world with happy faces again.

Epilogue

A year later.

Izzy curled on the couch, her head resting on Matthew's shoulder, Beau purring on her lap, and looked up at the painting of aunt Jemima and her family. So much had happened in the last year!

She was happy, she had a new relationship that was wonderful, the house was fully restored (using the surprisingly large sum that had come back from the bond at the retirement home), and there had been no further supernatural events since the day that she had read the letter in the hallway.

Well, not quite none. Every time she walked through the hall, or up the stairs, the air was warm and smelled of springtime – no matter what time of year it was. It reminded her, every time, to live life to the fullest, and forgive, and love.

She was going to do that, today, and every day hereafter.

About Raven Blackwood:

Raven Blackwood is an emerging author of classical ghost stories. To find out more about her work, visit her Facebook page and Website:

www.facebook.com/pg/RavenBlackwoodAuthor/

www.dreamstonepublishing.com/raven-blackwood-author/

Her novel The Haunting of Grove Manor is coming soon!

ABOUT THE AUTHOR

Lee Mountford was born and raised in the North East of England, in the small town of Ferryhill. Not much happens there, but it has a surprisingly dark history. This probably helped cultivate his love of horror.

He is an emerging author with a huge passion for the horror genre, and The Demonic is his second novel.

He still lives in the North East of England, with his amazing wife, Michelle. They are currently expecting their first child.

For more information

www.leemountford.com

leemountford01@googlemail.com

ACKNOWLEDGMENTS

Thanks first and foremost to my editor, Josiah Davis (http://www.jdbookservices.com), for such an amazing job.

The cover was supplied by Debbie at The Cover Collection (http://www.thecovercollection.com). I cannot recommend their work enough.

Thanks as well to fellow author—and guru extraordinaire—Iain Rob Wright for all of his fantastic advice and guidance. If you don't know who Iain is, remedy that now: http://www.iainrobwright.com. An amazing author with a brilliant body of work.

And the last thank you, as always, is the most important—to my amazing wife, Michelle. You are my world. Thank you for everything.

ISBN-13:

978-1974288373

ISBN-10:

1974288374

❀ Created with Vellum

Made in the USA
San Bernardino, CA
03 September 2017